D1132786

A gift of love...

...with a wish of joy and happiness to you, our Harlequin friends, now and in the coming year.

Harlequin has come a long way in its more than 30 years of publishing, and it's all because of you, our readers. So during this season of giving and loving we want to express our heartfelt thanks by sending you this gift of love—a beautiful romance novel by Violet Winspear. *Lucifer's Angel*, published in 1961, is her first Harlequin Romance, and one of her best.

Enjoy this moving love story. It comes with our warmest appreciation.

Sincerely,
Harlequin Reader Service
Christmas, 1980

For more than 30 years,
Harlequin has been
publishing the very best
in romantic fiction.

Today, Harlequin books
are the world's best-
selling paperback
romances.

LUCIFER'S ANGEL

by

VIOLET WINSPEAR

Harlequin Books

TORONTO • LONDON • LOS ANGELES • AMSTERDAM
SYDNEY • HAMBURG • PARIS • STOCKHOLM • ATHENS • TOKYO

Original hardcover edition published in 1961
by Mills & Boon Limited

ISBN 0-373-00593-8

Harlequin edition published 1961
Second printing January 1976
Third printing March 1976
Fourth printing May 1976
Fifth printing June 1976
Sixth printing May 1980
Seventh printing September 1980

Printed in U.S.A.

CHAPTER ONE

FAY sat gazing at the brand new wedding ring upon her finger — an exquisite ring, fashioned from platinum, with a band of small diamonds encircling it. The autumn sunshine danced in the stones, their glittering beauty filling her with panic rather than pleasure.

The seal that said she was now Lew Marsh's. The band that bound her to him!

She stole a tentative side-glance at him as he sat at the wheel of the car, weaving in and out of the heavy traffic of this Californian highway.

"We're too quiet," she thought. "We've just been married — we should at least be smiling."

"When will we get to the cabin, Lew?" she asked, for he had proposed that they honeymoon in a cabin he owned in the hills of Serena. She had agreed. But as she spoke, her tongue felt wooden, felt as though it hadn't uttered words for weeks. Not uttered words, when only a little while ago she had said, "I will!"

She knew sudden dread. It spread over her and touched her body with a paralyzing coldness. Why had she married him? It was a mistake. They'd never be happy. Look at him; he was so still, so withdrawn. She felt, all at once, desperately, miserably close to tears. Why had he married her, when he plainly felt no joy, no gladness — no anything?

He turned to look at her. "We'll be there by eight," he said. "You do want to go up to the cabin, don't you? I assure you it won't be running alive with spiders and damp rot." He grinned, a slightly derisive grin that lifted one corner of his wide, chiselled mouth and sent his left eyebrow in a mocking black peak. "It's quite a place, as a matter of fact. There's even a bathroom, though I admit the water has to be heated up on an oil stove."

"It sounds fine," she said.

"You said that as though it sounded dreadful," he reproved. "What's the matter?"

"Nothing."

"Oh, come on, something's wrong. You look a regular little ghost. Are you fed up with being married already?"

"Of course not." She twisted her beautiful ring round and round her finger. It felt heavy and strange on her finger, the diamonds glittered and danced — she wished — oh, she wished she didn't feel like bursting into tears!

"I bet I know what's the matter with you," Lew said. "You're hungry. Ten to one all you've had inside you all morning is a cup of coffee."

"I wasn't very hungry," she admitted.

"I knew it! First decent restaurant we see, we'll stop and have a meal. You'll feel fine, sweetheart, soon as you've had something to eat." He smiled at her and returned his attention to his driving.

Fay curled down more comfortably in her seat, forcibly pushing the thought of tears from her. There was no going back now. She was irrevocably married and to Lew Marsh.

Lew Marsh — a name to conjure within the world of film direction, for though only thirty-four, he already had several big successes to his credit. Lew Marsh, rapidly climbing the precarious Hollywood ladder of fame, choosing that she should accompany him — yet not from love — not from love.

When he had proposed to her, he had openly told

6

her that he wanted the marriage because he was tired of living alone.

"Will it work out, when you don't love me?" she had asked.

"Love!" He had laughed, contemptuously. "Shall I tell you about love? It's a pretty word they put on Valentine cards; an ingredient they stir into popular songs; a puff of air that's here one minute, gone the next. Don't ask me to give you pretty words, I'm not the type. Just take what I can give you, my admiration and my fondness; aren't they good, solid enough emotions for you?"

And because it had seemed a miracle to her that he should want her at all, she had, like a small, wistful bird, snatched at these crumbs of solace he offered. His admiration she couldn't quite believe in, for she was not a glamorous person. His fondness meant that he liked her unobtrusiveness; he could safely forget her whenever he wished, knowing that she wouldn't reproach him, knowing that she would slip quietly away to find some small amusement of her own until he should feel like beckoning her back to him again.

She loved him, of course. She had loved him from the first smile he had given her.

They had met at the house of his grandmother, where Fay had been nursing the irascible and very wealthy Mrs. Marsh.

Fay, who was English, had come to America two years before, when her widowed mother had died. She had come under a nursing exchange scheme and stayed to become a state registered nurse. This job, which she found far more interesting than hospital work, had taken her into quite a few homes and introduced her to many people. But right from her first day at Laurel Bay, she had been charmed and intrigued by the majestic irascibility of old Mrs. Marsh and the rather melancholy beauty of her grand-

7

daughter, Della, a young widow, who lived with her.

These people were different; and though Fay was no snob, she couldn't help appreciating the fact that Mrs. Marsh was the wealthiest woman in Casa Roche and that Della's brother was a well-known film director.

Then, one afternoon, he had arrived at the house. Old Mrs. Marsh had been rather sourly flattered that he should have come all the way from Hollywood on account of her gastric ulcer — until he had cynically informed her that he was really in Casa Roche on film business. He had had no idea that she was laid up with an ulcer. The carelessness with which he said this, actually in front of Fay, informed her that there was very little affection in his attitude toward his grandmother, although she had brought up both Lew and Della.

Their father had died when Della was two and Lew twelve. Their mother, an extremely beautiful but very unprincipled Sicilian, had remarried almost immediately. Her new husband had refused to accept the responsibility of her children, so she had callously deposited them on her mother-in-law's doorstep and carelessly dropped out of their lives forever.

Fay had learned all this from Della, for they had quickly become friends. They were both rather lonely people, linked by the loss of someone they had loved very dearly. Fay's loss was her mother; Della's, the young husband who had been killed in a car crash after only three months of marriage.

Fay and Della often talked during those long, warm August days, for Mrs. Marsh, despite her rather noisy bursts of temper at times, was a comparatively good patient; she slept a great deal, and it was during these hours that the friendship between Fay and Della warmed and deepened. It was upon Fay's advice, in fact, that Della finally agreed to marry Will Bronson, the engaging and gangling young lawyer whose

8

family's house adjoined the extensive grounds of Laurel Bay.

He was a persistent visitor at Laurel Bay and Fay quickly observed that he worshipped the tall, melancholy Della. "The man's crazy," Della said to Fay one afternoon, as they sat in the old rose arbor that stood in the grounds of Laurel Bay. "I wish he'd keep away."

"So that you can go on brooding," Fay had returned, with a flash of temerity that rather astounded her. Normally she wasn't a person to interfere in other people's affairs, but she liked both Della and Will; and she thought, with Mrs. Marsh, that if Della didn't find something to live for, she would develop into a dour recluse, wanting nothing but her own company and the painful memories of a boy who had been wild and reckless, though she had loved him.

"I couldn't ever love Will as I loved Philip," Della said then. "I should be cheating him."

"If you think that, then you're not completely indifferent to him, are you?" Fay returned.

Della smiled at that. "How come you're so wise, you young thing — you look about sixteen, do you know that?"

Old Mrs. Marsh was rapidly mending by then. That Sunday, to celebrate her recovery, the family had tea on the terrace. Fay was invited to the tea-party and joined it rather reluctantly. The sunshine was lush, the afternoon slow and filled with the movement of birds and the lazy fall of leaves from the tall trees in the garden of Laurel Bay. Old Mrs. Marsh, regal in black silk, presided over a teapot almost as regal as herself. Pleased as Punch that she could drink tea again, she was as full of pungent quips as her grandson, lounging at the table in gray flannels and a dark blue shirt and looking every bit as dangerous as a corsair in gleaming breastplate and helmet.

This was his tenth day in the house and still Fay was

overwhelmingly shy of him. When he spoke to her, she answered him in rather muffled monosyllables. When he smiled at her and his white teeth clenched on one of the dark cigars he smoked all the time, she thought she saw mockery in his smile and quick color would mount under the pale skin of her face and her throat. These reactions kept her sleepless at night. Men, until now, had been mere automatons with stethoscopes around their necks; she hadn't known that the world could hold a man like this one. Brazenly handsome as a jungle cat; boldly "damn your eyes and watch what you value" as any insolent cynical pirate. She suspected he was shockingly callous. He frightened her, yet he fascinated her. He made her want to run to him, yet he made her want to run away. She didn't know, until that afternoon upon the terrace, that she had fallen in love for the first time in her life.

It was as they drank tea, under a sky so blue and speckless it dazzled the eyes, that Della and Will announced their intention of marrying. Della, handsome in cream silk, blushed deeply as she made the announcement. The gangling Will looked like a kid with a dozen toys, while Mrs. Marsh nodded and chuckled with huge satisfaction.

Fay, sipping her tea, watched Lew. She saw sudden mischief flash in his dark eyes, saw his derisive grin break on his mouth. "We should be toasting this in champagne, but here goes!" He rose to his great height, and towering above the delicate ironwork of the terrace table, lifted his teacup to the blushing Della and the grinning Will. "Blessings on the union, my children, and don't you forget to call the first little blessing after me — always supposing you get the gender right." He drank off his tea with a flourish and had the mischievous satisfaction of receiving a scandalized glare from his grandmother.

"You're the limit, Lew Marsh!" she snapped. "Why

don't you go back to Hollywood, where you belong?"

"I am going back, my dear grandmother, just as soon as I've had my honeymoon."

"Had your what?"

"My honeymoon — those things people have when they get married." Very deliberately, then, he returned his teacup to its saucer, strolled round the table and pulled Fay up out of her seat. "Come for a walk with me," he said and marched her away from the table before she could draw breath to protest.

As he walked her under the trees of Laurel Bay, fear and perplexity made her heart race and thud in her side so that she had no defence against him when he suddenly stopped walking and pulled her into his hard brown arms. His lips were warm against her throat and she trembled in his arms, feeling she should fight him, yet not wanting to fight him. "You shouldn't do this — you shouldn't!" was all she found breath to say.

He laughed, softly, deeply. "I'm doing it, though. Want me to stop?"

"Yes."

"Little liar!" He took her lips then and Fay was lost. Like a small moth she fluttered in the dark flame of him and it mattered not that destruction might lie beyond the ecstasy he offered now. "Marry me and come to Hollywood with me," he said then. "I'm tired of living alone." He touched, coaxingly, the fairness of her hair, drew his finger down the delicate curve of her cheek, let it linger at the corner of her mouth. It was a truly lovely mouth, holding an ardent compassion and the sensitivity of the born dreamer; within the vivid blue of her eyes, she held still other dreams. She wasn't pretty, for her face was too quiet, but an elusive charm lurked about her; the appeal of delicate bones, soft voice and a rather childlike air of loneliness and vulnerability.

11

"But you don't love me, Lew," she said.

"Love!" He had laughed, contemptuously. . . .

They had reached the cabin at eight o'clock, just as Lew had said they would. The sun had died in a glorious flush of rose; now the sky was shot with lavender. A gentle autumnal breeze moved in the trees and the birds were clamorous at the approach of night.

Lew unlocked the door of the cabin and they carried in the two big bags of groceries they had bought in a town they had passed through that afternoon. Fay stood just inside the door, acutely conscious now that she was very much alone with Lew — Lew, who was her husband, but who was also a tall, dark stranger.

She felt dreamlike. She stood and breathed in a dream. She felt that she would awaken in a while and find that all this — Lew, her marriage, this cabin set among tall, aromatic trees and indescribably peaceful — was all just part of a dream.

She watched Lew stride forward into the shuttered gloom of the cabin, watched him put his bag of groceries down on a chair and throw wide the shutters over the two windows. Light shone into the room and Fay blinked, almost crying out in her bewildered delight.

Two big cream couches stood on either side of an immense open fireplace of red brick. In between them there gleamed a long, low coffee table. The black parquet floor was strewn with cream rugs, and the cream-painted walls were hung with a colorful miscellany of Indian artifacts. Against one wall stood an antique bureau, its wood dark and sheeny, and against another, a glass-fronted bookcase, crammed tight with books. It was a high, cool, pleasant room and Fay's eyes shone as she turned slowly to admire everything about it.

"Like it?" Lew enquired.

"I love it!" she exclaimed.

"No spiders, no damp rot, eh? Come on, I'll show you the kitchen."

She went with him, carrying her bag of groceries. When they entered the very neat and compact little kitchen, Lew took the bag from her and put it down on the table. He smiled as she absorbed, with astonished pleasure, the white cupboards, the white sink, the elaborate little oil stove.

"How come everything is so nice and clean?" she asked.

"A woman from a farm below comes up to clean and air the place for me," he told her. "I like it kept in the pink, because I occasionally drive up through the summer months."

"I see." She eyed the cupboards and with a knowing grin he opened one of them, revealing a wholesome supply of canned foods and fruits. "As you can see, we won't starve," he said. "In this other cupboard," he showed her, "I keep oil for the lamps and the stove. In here," again he showed her, "linen, cutlery and cooking pots. Now," he took hold of her hand and drew her from the kitchen, "now I'll show you the bedroom and the bathroom."

"The word 'cabin' hardly describes this place, Lew," she protested.

"Oh, I'm well aware of what you expected," he drawled, "some broken-down shack with two-tier bunks and a pump out back. My dear, you've got to get used to the idea that you haven't exactly married a penniless piper."

He squeezed her hand, and as her wedding ring pressed into her finger she was suddenly acutely conscious of how much the beautiful platinum band, completely encircled with diamonds, must have cost him. It must, she thought, have cost him a small fortune.

13

Her cheeks reddened and her glance fell away from his.

"Why the blush?" He drew her against his chest. "What's going on in that funny head of yours now?"

"You shouldn't have spent such a lot of money on my ring!" she blurted out. "You don't have to buy me, Lew."

"Buy you?" The smiling indulgence slowly died out of his face. "That's a great thing to say!" He took hold of her slender left hand and gazed down at the ring. "I thought the ring a pretty bauble; I thought you'd like it."

"I — I do — only it's such an expensive ring." She was acutely embarrassed, wishing she hadn't spoken.

He saw her embarrassment and suddenly he laughed, rather mockingly. "So I'm buying you, am I? Well, the buying won't end with a wedding ring, I assure you, my dear. Lew Marsh's wife wears silk, not holland aprons!" He swung on his heel with the words and went from the cabin to fetch their suitcases.

As dinner progressed, Lew's slight stiffness wore off. Fay was rather pleased with the dinner she had produced (this was, after all, the first time she had cooked on an oil stove), and she was gratified to see that Lew ate his dinner with gusto.

"You've a rare hand with a rare steak, my pet," he complimented her. "Who taught you to cook like this?"

"My mother. She was a wonderful cook."

"You were very fond of your mother, weren't you, Fay?" He poured himself a little wine, watching Fay as he drank it. "My mother was a witch!" he said deliberately. "A beautiful witch; hard as nails and selfish as well. Did you know that Gran thinks I take after my dear mother?"

Fay bit her lip at the sardonic amusement on his face. "I wish you wouldn't talk like that, Lew," she said. "You're always making yourself out as — as per-

14

fectly terrible. I think it's half the reason people think you are terrible."

"Oh, come now." He raised a mocking black brow at her, "You don't really think I'm a blue-eyed boy, sadly misunderstood, do you?"

"Well, I certainly don't think you're as bad as you make out." She rose and collected their plates and took them to the kitchen. She returned with dessert, a luscious-looking fruit salad topped with whipped cream. Lew eyed it with appreciation.

"You appear to possess all the virtues, my pet," he said. "Swell cook! Delicious smile. Optimistic nature!"

"How have I an optimistic nature?" she enquired, giving him a bit of the smile he labelled delicious.

"You did say, didn't you, that you don't think I'm quite as bad as I make out?"

"I did. And I believe it," she replied, biting into a stoned cherry.

"Now that's being optimistic."

"Lew, that's being cynical," she reproved.

After they'd had their coffee, they washed up the dishes and returned to the sitting room. Only one of the lamps was aglow, and the room looked pleasant and cosy. Lew had lit the fire — for the evenings, even the summer evenings, grew chilly this high in the hills — and the logs crackled and blazed, throwing out a sweet, piney scent.

"I do love this room!" Fay exclaimed, sitting down on one of the big cream couches and clasping her hands about her knees. "It's the sort of room one dreams about — you know. The sort of room I've always dreamed about, anyway."

"And what about the husband who goes with the room?" Lew enquired, sitting down on the other couch and taking out his cigar case. "Is he the sort of husband you've always dreamed about?"

Fay smiled slightly. As far as looks went, she reflected, he certainly met all the requirements of a dream husband!

"I never thought much about getting married," she confessed. "I never thought I would, as a matter of fact."

"Honey, haven't you ever taken a good look at yourself in a mirror?" he asked lazily.

She colored, watching him light his cigar. He tossed the match into the fire, lounged back in the couch, and comfortably stretched his legs. "Don't tell me I'm the first guy who's ever told you that you're a rather delectable little soul?" he drawled.

The pink of her cheeks deepened as she nodded her head.

"Incredible!" He smiled across at her. "And after Olive Hadley's had a go at you, you'll be prettier than ever."

"Who's Olive Hadley?" she asked.

"Olive, my pet, runs a very exclusive establishment in Hollywood where coltish young starlets go to be turned into elegant young ladies."

"Is that how you regard me, Lew, as a starlet?" she enquired, looking mischievous.

"You have such charming possibilities, and I'm naturally eager to see them fully exploited. Olive will style your hair for you, advise you on clothes and makeup. I might add that you certainly appear to need a little advice in that direction. That lipstick you're wearing is much too dark for your mouth."

"Is it?" She touched her mouth. "Is it really? It was very expensive." She remembered buying the lipstick in a lavender-draped shop in Casa Roche. "The girl said it suited me."

"Then she was color-blind!" He dismissed the girl with a disgusted flick of his wrist, spilling cigar ash on the carpet. "You've a singularly sweet mouth, Fay, and I don't like to see it daubed with a lipstick that was

16

designed exclusively for brunette business women. It hardens your mouth and detracts from the beauty of your eyes."

She gazed at him in a kind of stunned wonder. Her mouth sweet! Her eyes beautiful!

He laughed. "It's easy to see you're not used to receiving compliments. Stop looking so amazed. You've a stunning mouth, you've nice eyes. Why shouldn't I say so?"

"Oh, I don't mind!" she assured him, smiling. She laid her head back against the soft cushioning of the couch, a relaxed happiness coursing its way through her. It was very pleasant, even exciting, to be told that one had a stunning mouth and a nice pair of eyes. Especially by Lew. Most especially by Lew.

"Tell me about yourself, Fay," he said lazily, "Where did you live when you were a kid?"

"A rather drab part of London called Holloway." She wrinkled her nose. "We lived in a two-roomed flat that always seemed to smell of other people's cooking and was always full of other people's noises. My mother worked in a hot little factory there. It was her idea that I take up nursing; she so dreaded the thought of my working in a factory. After she died and I finished my training, I went in for private nursing." She smiled a little. "I wanted to see other places — see something of the world."

"Via other people's sick-rooms?" Lew drawled. His eyes, in that moment, were curiously gentle, and Fay was confused — startled that he should look like that.

"I suppose — I suppose that does sound a little silly," she admitted. "But private nursing isn't a bad sort of job, not when you've got to earn your own living. And you do move around a bit."

"D'you think you'll enjoy your new job?" He was smiling as he leaned forward to flick cigar ash into the fire. The smile seemed to travel down her slender, relaxed body in the big couch and linger on her delicate ankles. "Well?" he insisted.

Moved to shyness by his glance, she turned her face against the soft cushioning of the couch, avoiding his eyes. "I already like my new job," she murmured. "Though I must admit my new boss scares me just a little. He will keep looking at my ankles."

She heard him laugh. "My dear," he said, "the time to get scared is when he stops looking. You bear that in mind."

The room fell quiet, pleasantly redolent of the piney scent of the purring logs and the aromatic richness of Lew's cigar. The clock ticked softly, and the steady, hypnotic grating of crickets stole in from outside. Fay's eyes drooped and closed contentedly. She could feel the warmth of the fire stealing down her legs, the luxurious softness of the couch like an embrace. She snuggled more closely into that embrace — and drifted into sleep with the ease and naturalness of a child.

She awoke about an hour later — sat up, feeling bemused and rather ashamed of herself. How dreadful, to have fallen asleep like that on Lew! She sat rubbing her eyes, gazing at the opposite couch, no longer occupied by his dark, lounging figure. She rose and wandered out to the kitchen, thinking he might be making himself a sandwich, perhaps. But he wasn't. She looked in the bedroom, but it was quite empty. When she knocked on the door of the bathroom, only silence answered her.

She stood with one hand at her throat, her eyes enormous as alarm darted through her. Where had he gone? Why had he left her? Had she annoyed him, falling asleep like some six-year-old stuffed too full of joy-riding and whipped cream?

She hurried back to the sitting room, crossed to the front door, and opened it. A chill night breeze blew in at her, a somber darkness greeted her. All she could

18

hear at first were the crickets, and then she became aware of other noises. The low, weird hoot of an owl, the rustling of wind-tossed leaves and queer little scuttlings, as of small night creatures scrambling in the dark.

As she stood in the doorway of the cabin, gazing into the darkness, she felt an indescribable loneliness. The redwood trees, so high, wide and handsome with the sun on them, were great menacing shapes now that seemed to have drawn very close to the cabin.

Fear touched her, moved on her skin like clammy fingers, and she drew back into the cabin, slamming the door, shutting out the lonely, crowding darkness. She stood with her back to the door, her heart hammering. Where was Lew? Why had he left her alone? So alone, up here in the hills, with only the darkness and the monster trees to keep her company?

CHAPTER TWO

FAY moved woodenly across the room to the dying fire. She crouched down in front of it, encompassed by a quiet so intense that even the rustling of her dress seemed to intrude on it. She stared into the fallen, sombre heart of the fire, one hand clenched hard against her hammering heart.

Panic slowly receded and the return of calmness brought things back into proper perspective. Lew would saunter back from his nocturnal stroll in due course, careless of whether or not it had frightened her to awaken to silence and loneliness. A reluctant smile hovered about her mouth. Love for Lew had not blinded her to his failings. She knew him for what he was, an imperious, swaggering pirate of a man who went his own way; reaching out decisively for what he wanted, rejecting, without a moment's hesitation what he didn't want. Superbly, arrogantly free of petty fear or petty disapproval; neither a gentle man nor a patient one, his temper would create a small hell for her should she ever arouse it.

Yet she loved him — and beneath her fear, thrilling along her nerves, there suddenly sprang into being a primitive gladness that she awaited his coming, that she wore his ring — that she belonged to him.

Then, outside in the night, she suddenly heard twigs break as feet trod them; heard those feet come closer and mount the cabin steps. Very slowly she stood up and the hand that lay over her heart felt its mad racing. She turned toward the door, watching as the latch dipped, watching as the door swung inward, watching, like a small, ensnared bird, the arrival of Lew. Her pale hair lay ruffled on her forehead, the lemon silk of her dress lay away from the delicate fragility of her throat, and her mouth was very lovely and very vulnerable, offering love, but begging him to understand her slight fear.

He closed the door and came across the room to her, immensely tall in the gloom of the room, and Fay was held motionless, ensnared in his eyes. They were intent on her as he came for her, reaching out his brown hands and gathering her to him. With a small gasp, she accepted the hard possession of his embrace, pressing her face to him. "Where did you go?" she whispered. "Everything was so quiet — so quiet!"

He took her chin in his hand and lifted it, studying her face, a faint smile playing about his mouth. "I strolled down to see Mrs. Pascoe, the woman who comes in to clean this place. She and her husband have a farm about half a mile down. Were you frightened, Fay? I hoped you'd go on sleeping till I got back."

Her hands gripped his shoulders. "I didn't know what to think. I didn't know where you'd gone."

His smile deepened. "Did you think I'd run out on you? Do I look the sort of guy who'd run out on his bride on his wedding night?" His arms tightened about her and his eyes, gazing down into hers, were very dark, with tiny sparkles caught way down in their depths. Fay was held fascinated by them as Lew lowered his head toward her. Then they were lost to her as he pressed his warm cheek to hers. "Shy of me, Fay?" he whispered.

"A little," she confessed.

"You don't have to be, you know." His lips lightly touched her cheek. Then he swung her up into his arms and as he carried her from the room, Fay laid her face against the hard warmth of his throat, feeling

21

his soft laughter vibrate under her cheek. "What a featherweight you are!" he murmured. "I could wear you in my buttonhole."

"Like one of Della's carnations?" she enquired, smiling against his throat. Della hadn't liked him wearing her carnations, especially her pale yellow prize-winners, but he had played vandal on more than one occasion, cocking an insolent eyebrow at Della when she flew into a tantrum to see one of her "pets" gaily decorating his buttonhole.

"Ouch!" His laughter deepened. "Don't scold me on my wedding night, sweetheart."

For an answer, Fay kissed his cheek.

They stayed two weeks at Serena.

They hiked in the hills, fished in the lakes, boated and swam and ate huge farmhouse teas with the friendly Pascoes. And Fay forgot to worry about the future. She dismissed the future. She was too happy with the here and now.

The hills of Serena were peaceful — their sweeping dips and gracefully curving upsweeps dappled with the glorious tints of autumn. Fay knew that she would remember Serena all her life. And when Lew said to her, at the end of their two weeks, "Well, we start for home tomorrow. I've got to get back to work," she murmured a quiet goodbye to those rolling hills beyond the windows of the cabin; said goodbye to the peace and contentment they had brought her. Now tomorrow loomed and though she held her small chin high, she quailed a little at the thought of Hollywood.

Hollywood, with its brazen skies and its stretching, golden beaches; its sophistication and its glamor; its black heartbreak for some; its glittering, neon adulation for others.

She must step forth into this glistening whirlpool and accept with equanimity, if she could, the stares

22

and the comments and the amazement. Oh yes, there would be amazement! She didn't doubt it for one moment. But she carried her small chin bravely and smiled when Lew announced their imminent departure from Serena. "Had fun, my sweet?" he asked.

"I've loved it here," she said. "I've loved every second, every hour!"

Three days later, Lew's car drew to a standstill in the smoothly gravelled, circular drive of the exclusive Crystal Court in Hollywood, where Lew had his apartment. Fay gazed at the handsome white building in nervous awe. The feeling was undiminished as she crossed the quiet lobby with Lew, rode with him to the top floor in a lift that moved with the silence and ease of a bird.

They stepped out into a lushly carpeted corridor with wide windows at either end, through which the afternoon sun streamed blindingly. While Lew searched his pockets for the key to the apartment, Fay stood at one of the windows, gazing down big-eyed upon a vista of wide, clean avenues. Exotic, thick-stemmed palm trees marched like sentinels along the curb edges, and big houses stood in secluded gardens of gleaming camellia bushes and lemon trees.

She jumped when Lew spoke to her, whirling from the window and moving tentatively to take the hand he held out to her. The sunshine followed her, turning her hair to a delicate fairness and playing over the blue linen of her dress. She felt Lew's warm fingers close over her cold ones as he drew her into the apartment that was to be her home.

It was large and cool and very, very modern, with a lovely brilliant blue carpet flowing to the soft gray of the walls. Exotic cacti stood in scarlet pots and a great white couch spread with scarlet cushions sat in the corner. A lush, exciting, film-like place — frightening the life out of Fay. She had never, in all her twenty-three years, known anything like it; alien and elegant and many miles removed from the threadbare little flat she had shared with her mother. How sadly lacking in glamor and luxury that poor little place had been!

"Well, come on," Lew suddenly said, "show a little enthusiasm!"

She kept her eyes turned from him, answering with care: "It's a lovely place, Lew."

He watched her, saw her hands clench on her white handbag, and his lips twitched with sudden irritation. She looked — why, she looked almost scared! What the devil was there to be scared about?

He stepped across the room to her and took hold of her slim shoulders. "What are you scared about?" he asked.

"I'm not scared," she denied.

"You're scared stiff! You're imagining this room filled with my friends and you're trembling in your shoes. What the heck do you think they'll do to you — eat you?"

She ceased pretending. She nodded miserably. "They'll bite lumps out of me. They'll think me an awful bumpkin."

"They will if you're going to behave like one," he agreed. "If you're going to act like a stranger in your own home, people are going to snicker and talk."

"But I feel such a stranger!" she burst out, "I — I —" But she couldn't tell him. She couldn't say, "I feel so afraid, Lew. All this is so exotic, so unlike anything I've ever known. You've got to give me time to get used to it. Accept my fear, Lew. Accept it and it will soon die." She couldn't say it, for he wouldn't understand. He was so completely without fear or reserve himself that he had little or no patience with these things in other people.

"I expect I shall soon get used to everything," she

24

said, her smile careful, her heart apprehensive, the confidence she had known at Serena suddenly stripped from her.

"Let's hope so!" he retorted.

So, with mixed feelings of trepidation and excitement, Fay settled down to married life in Hollywood.

However, married life was filled with a bewildering amount of leisure for a girl who had worked as a nurse since the age of seventeen. Hardly any domesticity was demanded of her, for the cleaning of the apartment was dealt with by the management of Crystal Court; while Lew's only call upon her cooking capabilities was for a breakfast each morning, before he left for the studios. In the evenings they always went out to dine — an arrangement that appealed less and less to Fay as the days passed.

It seemed so silly to her that they should eat dinner in noisy, crowded restaurants each evening when she was a perfectly good cook and the apartment possessed a glittering, gadget-packed kitchen. Why should it be used only once a day?

Finally she decided to attack the arrangement and Lew arrived home from work one evening to find her setting out the table in the dining room, carefully arranging flowers, table-mats, and tall red candles. She had bought new holders that day.

Lew's decisive stride into the dining room was checked as he took note of what she was doing. "What's all this in aid of?" he demanded. "Are we expecting company?"

Fay turned to smile at him, a smile that was cheery, with just a slight edge of nervousness to it. "Oh, I thought it would be rather nice if we had dinner at home for once," she replied. She moved toward him, her fingers caught in the gay frill edging her apron. "Do you mind?" she asked.

He didn't answer for a second or two, his eyes flickering up and down her small, aproned figure. His mouth thinned. "You look like a damned domestic!" he snapped. "Get that thing off and quit acting the sweet suburban bride — we're going out!"

Fay flinched at the hard edge to his voice, while her eyes travelled warily over his face. Bad temper showed in every chiselled line of it. "Had a stiff day, Lew?" she asked.

"Yeah!" He swung away from her and poured himself a drink at the sideboard. "I've had exactly three blazing rows today, and I'm feeling as mean as Satan." He tossed down his drink. "Those fools in publicity are kicking up a fuss because I want Connie Carr in *Corn In The City*. They've gone all Puritan Fathers on me because she was mixed up in a divorce case about three months ago. So what! The woman can act. Who cares about what she likes to do after working hours — I'm sure I don't! She's a cinch for this film, Fay; got a lazy Alabama drawl, corn-colored hair to her waist, and a mouth that's all sex and spite."

"What happened, Lew? Did you manage to persuade the people in publicity to let you have her?" A sudden little smile, that she was quite unable to suppress, played about the curves of Fay's mouth as she pictured the chaos that had probably reigned in the publicity offices today. She was learning that this man kicked against being curbed with the untamed ferocity of a roped stallion; and like a roped stallion, he could be full of damage and danger when the mood was upon him.

He saw her smile and joined it with an irritated laugh.

"I've got her, but I came close to bouncing Bellamy Taylor down the garbage shoot. He's the guy who handles most of the stories that are put out about our contract stars; a fat little slug with restless hands! He was

26

grinding his heel down on Connie and I happen to know a couple of kids who've had some unfortunate dealings with the guy; I casually mentioned their names, and that lifted his heel off Connie!" Lew was looking quizzical as he approached Fay and tipped up her chin. "Sorry about your dinner arrangements, pet, but I want music and noise tonight."

"But, Lew, I've got a chicken in the oven!" she protested.

He looked quite unmoved. "That's your worry, not mine." He turned from her and made for the bedroom, dragging off his tie as he went.

Fay ran after him, catching at his arm. "You're being awfully unreasonable, Lew." Her face, raised to his, was beseeching. "Is it such a big thing to ask of you, that we stay home this one night and eat in our own home?"

"Look," his expression became haughty, "I work hard all day long and I happen to appreciate a little gaiety in the evenings. I'm mighty sorry if this doesn't quite meet with your prim approval, Mrs. Marsh, but you'll have to get used to pampering my somewhat Bohemian likes and dislikes, or we're going to have these tiresome battles every night of the week. I'm no domestic animal, my dear; I never made out to be one, so stop trying to get the tiger to lie down on the kitchen mat — it won't work!" He shook off her hand and made for the bathroom, tossing his tie and his jacket on the bed as he went.

Fay stood indecisively in the doorway. He was in a temper and it was probably silly of her to persist in her argument, but she had taken such pains with their dinner. Right now the chicken was turning a beautiful golden brown and the ice-box held peaches in jelly and ice cream. "Such a pity — to waste a perfectly good dinner," she murmured.

Lew glanced back at her as he was disappearing into

the bathroom. "We'll eat cold fowl for breakfast. I'm game," he drawled.

"And cold baked potatoes and asparagus heads?" she queried.

"Giving in?" He shot a grin at her over his shoulder, that wicked left eyebrow of his a taunting black arch, a deliberate outward sign of the vein of cynical independence that ran in his blood. "Afraid that I'll dine and dance some cute young thing if you don't come out with me? You know that I'm perfectly capable of doing just that, don't you?"

And that remark, so carelessly, yet so flagrantly spoken, touched off rebellion in Fay, woke her quiet spirit to a flash of sheer anger. He was so sure of her! So sure that she didn't dare cross him. So sure, and so amused that she held their marriage like a precariously balanced and extremely delicate glass bowl, a continuous fear in her that she would drop that bowl and their marriage would smash. With passionate dignity, her small frame drawn up tautly as she faced him, she said, "Get your little bit of gaiety by all means, Lew. Dine and dance half a dozen blondes if you wish. I'll stay at home and eat my very nice dinner. Then I'll curl up with a book and not say a word when you come in with blonde hairs on your tuxedo."

With these words, she turned and marched away to the kitchen, feeling rather pleased with herself.

But Fay's pleasure had melted right away by one-thirty, when, for the fourth time, she had switched on the bedside lamp and apprehensively examined the impassive face of the small clock that ticked on the bedside table. She ran restless hands through her hair, then slid down in the big bed, pulling the silk coverlet to her chin.

Lew's independence was so inviolable a thing; a hard glaze about him that couldn't be damaged or softened by love, as hers must inevitably be. She felt shattered now by their fight; she felt it was all her fault. It was so much easier, so much less painful in the end to give in to him, for all he really asked of her was that she be his distraction at the end of his long, pressing day at the studios. It was a mistake to play at being the keeper of his home. She was not that. She was just one more ornament he had added to it, something to be picked up and admired at his pleasure; and — she felt this to be true — something to be set aside and forgotten. . . .

Then she stiffened in the bed, for there were sudden footsteps in the sitting room, the careless sound of Lew whistling a certain airy tarantella he was fond of. Fay lay very still. He might think she slept. He must think she slept! She shrank from the thought of him finding her still awake, obviously thinking, worrying — wanting him.

The bedroom door opened and closed and his cheery whistling approached the bed. The lamp clicked on, bathing Fay in its pool of rose-pink light. She knew that Lew was watching her, waiting for her to turn and speak to him. But she wouldn't. He must be the one to capitulate. Her whole body ached for his capitulation.

"Fay?" He spoke softly. "Fay, are you asleep?"

She didn't move, but he seemed to know instinctively that she was still awake. With a soft little laugh he sat down on the bed and reached for her, pulling her out of the bedcovers and into his arms. His lips quirked as he examined her rebellious face, drawing a teasing finger down her cheek. "Well," he drawled, "aren't you going to ask me where I've been and what I've been doing?"

"I don't know whether I dare." Her eyes met his with defiance.

"Afraid of a lie or the truth?" He was laughing

openly at her, his teasing, travelling finger now at one
of the lacy straps of her nightdress.

"Afraid of both, I suppose," she admitted, shivering
slightly at his touch, inwardly contemptuous of her
own weak susceptibility to him.

He laughed. "Don't you want to examine my tuxedo
for blonde hairs?"

She shook her head, flinching from the mockery in
his eyes — his eyes that openly said that it was entirely immaterial to him whether or not her eyes
discovered blonde hairs upon his tuxedo. A sharp little
arrow of pain pierced her and as pain spread through
her, her face went forward against his warm, hard
throat. He blew at the soft hair falling childishly on to
her forehead, and a tinge of curiosity moved in his
eyes as they travelled over her, taking in the delicate
modelling of her shoulders, the perfect arching of her
small feet, peering out from the hem of her blue nightdress. She seemed good, but was she good, this small
thing with her ardent mouth and her heart racing like
a mad thing under his hand? Was she good, or was she
like all other women, treacherous and shallow beneath
the outward softness and sweetness? When those
curling lashes hid the blue eyes, as they hid them now,
what secret thoughts was she having that he must not
read?

"Look at me, Fay," he suddenly commanded.

But her face pressed closer into his throat and he
felt a little tremor go through her. "I don't like us to
quarrel," she whispered. "Let's stop it, Lew — please!"

"It hurts, does it?" He took her chin in his hand,
forcing her to look at him, holding her helpless and
small across his arm. The gold hair spread against
the darkness of his tuxedo and the soft blue of her
nightdress threw into relief the soft whiteness of her
skin. She looked, Lew thought, his lips curving upon a
smile that bordered upon the sadistic in that moment,

30

like a trapped butterfly. "Listen to me," he said. "When a guy takes as much temperament as I do, taming a bunch of wildcat actors and actresses all day long, he doesn't want it dished up in his own home. So cut out the temperament — I won't have it!" Then, with easy strength, he returned her to her warm little nest in the big bed and drew the coverlet up about her chin. "How was the chicken?" he asked.

"Horrible." She tentatively smiled at him, willing him to smile back, without mockery. Willing a show of tenderness from him, even though it was that lazy tenderness for a toy that he sometimes showed her. Even that — even that might banish in some measure the heartache of this evening.

But he didn't smile and her heart jolted at the curious way he suddenly examined her, his eyes travelling her face with a searching, almost startled intentness. Then, with a peremptory hand, he pushed the tumbled hair back from her forehead, brushed it smooth, bringing the delicate pointed contours of her face into an abrupt definition, which the usual soft waving of her hair about her ears and her forehead was inclined to blur. Lew studied this effect for perhaps a minute. Then, with a quiet oath, he swung from the bed and strode to the dressing-table, where he stood removing his cuff links.

Fay watched him with puzzled eyes, nerves jumping sharply under her skin as he tossed the cuff links down and they bounced on the smooth surface of the dressing-table, cutting the silence that lay over the room. "What's the matter now, Lew?" she asked, quietly.

"Nothing," he retorted, but Fay, watching his wide shoulders, saw them tauten, as though they braced to take a sudden weight.

"I — I think there is." She half sat up, the silk coverlet slipping from her shoulders, leaving their

31

young, thin whiteness to pick up delicate fingers of shadow from the rose-pink light of the bedside lamp. Lew could see her through the mirror of the dressing table, and the pupils of his eyes expanded. Even as her youthful delicacy, still strange and new in his bed, in his home, stirred possession awake in him, he turned to her with a mouth gone tight and grim. "All right, if you must know! You're inclined to look like — someone I used to know! Now let's drop the subject, shall we?"

"Someone — someone you used to know?" Her eyes were large and troubled and achingly blue. The tension and the antagonism that lay between herself and Lew was a very real pain at her quickly beating heart. Oh, this tension had to be shattered, had to be broken, or it would break her. With a sudden throwing off of reserve, a sudden abandonment to woman's infinitely greater capacity to forgive, if not to forget, she threw out her arms to Lew. It didn't matter in this moment that he hadn't told her, plainly had no intention of telling her, where and with whom he had spent the long hours of her tormented evening. "Oh, Lew, a little bit of your past?" she asked, and she even managed to laugh a little.

He stood tall and haughty before her, watching with a cold speculation the play of rose-pink shadow along the white curving of her outstretched arms. Then, with a careless, arrogant laugh, he came to her arms, felt them close softly about his neck. "Yeah, a little bit of my past," he rejoined, burying his lips against rose-pink shadow in the hollow of her throat, where nervous little pulses raced under the increasing pressure of his lips.

32

CHAPTER THREE

"YEAH, a little bit of my past," Lew had said, and in the days that followed, those words were often with Fay, a persistent undertow, running dangerous and dark beneath the effervescent froth of the Hollywood whirlpool.

She knew that they signified another woman — she also knew that that woman had helped to make Lew the hard, careless person he very often was.

So now she watched when they attended parties, or sat in restaurants and cinemas, watched for a face that might possess something of the look of her own face, but though there were many faces at these parties, in these restaurants, the one she searched for continued to elude her.

In her single days, when she had been neat, sometimes harried, but always efficient Nurse Bryan, she had, along with all the other hundreds of working girls seeking a little color and escape from the daily rush and routine of earning bread and board, read of Hollywood in the glossy film magazines. Read of its gaiety, its many parties. . . .

The parties did exist — mad whirls, noisy vortexes, where all manner of film people gathered in animated groups and talked about anything and everything connected with films. These parties might, Fay often thought, be the bread of life to anyone connected with the mad, mad business of making films, but she found them bewildering and lonely. She was outside the magic circle, even forgotten by Lew when film cronies carried him off to a far corner, where he would often remain for the rest of the evening, immersed in film talk, lost to her existence.

Yet it was at one of these gatherings that Fay met Cleo Nixon, the woman who was to become the first real friend Fay made in Hollywood.

Cleo, it turned out later, was the wife of a brilliant young cameraman at the same studios where Lew worked, and she and Fay liked one another from the moment Cleo had her elbow jogged and very nearly distributed the entire and rather vegetable contents of a tall cocktail over Fay's head. With a merry peal of laughter she saved the glass, pulling such a comically malignant face at the man who had so carelessly jogged her elbow that Fay's glance of alarm turned to one of quick amusement instead.

Cleo, gratified by Fay's amusement, stayed to perch herself on the arm of Fay's chair. Within minutes they were exchanging Christian names and were openly confessing to a mutual unappreciation of these smart crushes.

"They're awful, aren't they?" Cleo exclaimed, chasing a piece of cucumber around her drink with a small pointed stick. "I only come because Ted has to kind of keep up with everything. If you're ambitious, it doesn't do to sit at home and wait for opportunities to come knocking on the door. It's at do's like these that important contacts are made. That's Ted." She pointed with her little stick at a rather tubby, gesticulating young man in horn-rimmed spectacles, who was in deep and earnest conversation with a long-faced, executive type, whom Fay guessed to be one of the important contacts Cleo spoke about.

"Ted can talk till the cows come home when the mood's on him," Cleo went on, her glance openly affectionate as it rested on the tubby young man. "Look at him sounding off there!" She giggled as her glance came again to Fay. "We're a pair, really, we both like to talk, yet we've a little boy who's as solemn as a church bell." She eyed Fay with candid, pert interest. "You seem a little out of all this, if you don't mind my saying so. You're new to Hollywood, aren't you?"

Fay nodded. "I'm from England."

"Are you now!" Cleo's brandy-brown eyes expressed a heightened interest. "Do you like Hollywood?" she asked.

"I — I'm not sure, to tell you the truth." Fay's smile moved tentatively on her gentle mouth. Could she tell this girl what she couldn't tell Lew, that Hollywood was inclined to frighten the life out of her? That most of the people she met at these parties chilled her to the marrow with their glittering audacity and their determined ambitions? Fears she could not confide to Lew! A week ago they had attended a big charity dance, a swarming affair of raining balloons, popping champagne corks and skittish dresses that looked as though they wouldn't last out the night, and Fay continued to remember Lew's words to her when they had finally left the dance in the early hours of the morning: "My stars, you might look as though you're enjoying yourself when I take you out, Fay. Tonight you looked just like some Christian martyr, about to be rent by lions." He had laughed, but his laughter had held more annoyance than amusement. Fay had known, then, that she could never turn to him with her fears.

Now, watching Cleo, she knew an urge to confide in her, yet loyalty to Lew held her back. All she said was, "The climate's glorious, isn't it? And I've never eaten so much fruit in my life."

"So that accounts for your stunning skin," Cleo returned, pertly grinning at Fay's quick blush. Her eyes moved to the glittering wedding ring on Fay's finger. "You haven't been married for very long, have you?" she said, spearing a cherry out of her drink and

35

chewing it with dainty pleasure. She smiled at Fay. "You've got bride written all over you. Who's the lucky guy?"

Fay glanced round the room, searching for Lew's tall figure. She saw him over in a window embrasure, very dark against a background of cream silk curtains, a cigar clamped between his teeth as he frowned and talked to a striking-looking woman of indeterminate age, whom Fay recognized as Claire Remay. It struck her as a trifle awe-inspiring that her husband should be talking to this extremely famous star in such an intent fashion.

"There he is," she said to Cleo, a twinkle in her eye as she awaited Cleo's reaction. She didn't go unrewarded. Cleo's mouth fell open and she gave a low, startled whistle. "You're married to Lew Marsh!" she exclaimed. "Well, button up my high, shiny boots! Who'd have believed it!" She stared at Fay. "Let me offer you my condolences," she added cryptically.

Fay laughed. She liked this girl too much to be offended by her impertinence. "It's the cigar," she returned, lightly. "He always looks stern and big-business with one of those things between his teeth. You should see him with marmalade on his mouth."

"He eats marmalade?" Cleo was staring across at Lew. There were many stories about this man and he always, in her opinion, looked every one of them. It struck her as rather grim that this sweet kid, in the peach dress that made her look sixteen, should be tied up to him. He was such a forbidding-looking brute; so darned arrogant — so much the "monarch of all I survey" type. Not cuddly and easy like Ted.

"He looks like he eats babes like you for breakfast," she laughed. "I can almost see him spreading on the jam and munching you up in those fierce, white teeth."

The tentative dimples below the delicate thrusting

36

of Fay's cheekbones came and went. "You're being most disrespectful about one of Hollywood's most sought-after film directors," she reproved.

"Does he direct you?" Cleo was watching Fay over the rim of her cocktail glass, and though she smiled, sympathy lurked in her smile. "No, don't answer that," she suddenly added. "You don't have to."

"Don't I?" Fay touched the shining stones encircling her wedding ring and her somewhat embarrassed glance withdrew from the knowledge upon Cleo's pert face, settling again upon Lew. Now he and Claire Remay had been joined by a tall fair man wearing a rather untidy suit of plum-colored corduroy. Fay smiled to see him. She liked Bill Symans, with his rather distant blue eyes and the rather old-fashioned courtliness he showed to all women. He was a writer, and though he and Lew appeared to have very little in common, they were close friends. She said to Cleo, "Do you know Bill Symans?"

"Who doesn't?" Cleo's exclamation was warm. "The guy's a saint! I bet if you had a census to find the most popular person in Hollywood, Bill Symans would top the list. He's never too tired or too busy to help someone out of a spot of bother and as fast as he makes money out of those fabulous novels of his, he gives it away."

"And in the true tradition of a saint, he will die young," Fay murmured.

Cleo glanced at her sharply. "What do you mean?" she asked.

"He's a sick man. Lew told me."

"Oh, no!"

"He has a heart condition, and there is no known cure."

"Bill Symans, of all people!" Cleo's small sun-tanned hands folded tight about the tall glass that held her cocktail. "No wonder — no wonder his eyes always

37

have that strange far away look in them — as though he already glimpses heaven." Then Cleo suddenly stopped. "Let's talk about my little boy," she exclaimed. "We're getting morbid."

"I'd love to talk about your little boy," Fay said at once. "Is he like you?"

"Not in the least. . . ."

Fay began to see a lot of Cleo Nixon after that party. The big apartment was very empty during the day, with Lew gone from it so many hours, and Fay welcomed Cleo's entertaining company.

They toured the exciting Hollywood shops together and Fay, who was provided with an amazingly generous allowance by Lew, found that it was a truly delightful feeling to be able to saunter into one of these fabulous shops and buy herself an extravagantly crazy hat or a bottle of deliciously expensive perfume.

And when Fay didn't want to go shopping, Cleo took her sightseeing, showing her the elegant, secluded homes of the big stars. One house she saw was the one-time home of the famous screen star, Astra James. Now it stood empty and neglected in a garden of tall weeds and brambled hedges. The house intrigued Fay to such an extent that she and Cleo finally scrambled through an opening in the iron railings surrounding the garden and crept cautiously through the weeds to peer in at the lower windows of the house.

The drawing room loomed long and lofty and sadly dirty before their eyes, the huge marble fireplace and the painted ceiling, depicting half-clad wood nymphs fleeing before the tempestuous thunder of fiercelooking centaurs. They were the only reminders left of the past glamor this house had known.

"Can't you just see Astra James draped against that mantelpiece?" Cleo whispered. "Gold lamé clinging to her from her throat to her heels, her eyes painted up

38

and a brandy glass held elegantly in one of her hands?"

Fay nodded. "Whatever became of her? She was awfully famous at one time, wasn't she?"

"She went broke, I think. Anyway, she quit Hollywood years ago. She had too much of everything, I reckon. Too much beauty, too many men; it all probably got the better of her in the end. Perhaps she married some sweet, tame guy and settled down quietly in the backwoods with him."

"After being so famous! Do you really think she could do that?" Fay looked doubtful. "Could gold lamé be exchanged for starched gingham, do you think?"

Cleo shrugged and traced a solemn profile in the grime covering the window. "This is a mighty funny world, honey lamb, and people are mighty funny creatures," she said, reflectively. "There's no knowing what we'll do when we're pushed into a corner. We might whimper, we might pass out cold, we might fight like crazy. Then again we might run. There's just no knowing. For my book, Astra James ran off and found herself a little peace, far from the mad noise of Hollywood."

Fay and Cleo also spent a great deal of time down on the beach. Along with Cleo's small son, Eric, they ran and played energetically in the glorious October sunshine that still persisted.

Eric wasn't a bit like his mother. He was a serious-eyed blond child, and other people on the beach were inclined to mistake him for Fay's son. Cleo said to her one day, after a woman had pried Eric's blond head out from under his sand bucket and brought him to Fay, telling him to stay by his "momma" and fill his bucket with sand instead of head, "You must be the maternal type, Fay. People are always taking you for Eric's mother. You ought to have a baby."

Fay colored. She liked children and they liked her, but she didn't think, somehow, that they were included in Lew's plans. But Cleo, taking quick, amused note of her blush, misunderstood. "Don't tell me you're already having one?" she twinkled.

Fay shook her head.

"Oh, well," Cleo lounged back on her elbow, watching Fay as she caught Eric into her arms, bending her fair head to his, "perhaps it's just as well. Your Lew isn't like my Ted. You know where you are with Ted's sort, ordinary, down-to-earth, but Lew Marsh is so darned handsome! Don't you get scared, Fay? Don't you worry all the time? I know I should, that's why I say thank God for Ted; I know he'll never cause me any sort of — of women worry."

"I don't — think about what tomorrow might bring," Fay replied carefully, tickling Eric's ribs and rolling him in the sand, turning her pink face from the friendly curiosity of Cleo's eyes.

"Why did you marry the guy?" Cleo pursued. "I know he's darned attractive and all the rest, but he looks as though he'd be an arrogant brute to live with. Whereas you're such a gentle, good-hearted kid." She filtered the glistening sand through her fingers. "I think you're a whole lot too good for him, if you want my opinion," she burst out bluntly.

Fay glanced at her, smiling a little. "Did I come as a very great shock to everybody?" she asked.

Cleo grinned. "Everybody says he's either nuts or nuts about you. Which is it?"

"Which do you think it is?" Fay countered.

Cleo studied her, her fine-boned face and body, her large eyes that were candid yet shy, her mouth that was ardent and yet gentle. Perhaps, Cleo thought, Fay would appeal to the brute in Lew Marsh — someone soft and innocent for him to hypnotize with his charm and then break. He had, it appeared, grown tired of breaking the more experienced type of female.

"Fay," she said, with a sudden touch of urgency,

"please be careful. Don't love that guy too much."

Fay stared at her. "Why do you say that?" she asked.

Cleo shrugged her shoulders. "Oh — I just think he's as hard as nails. I shouldn't like to see him hurt you; he's capable of it. His sort always is. They — use women, but they don't love them. They've a sort of fundamental contempt for women. Haven't you noticed?"

"Perhaps." Fay turned her eyes toward the sea, gazing fixedly at its blueness, the dazzling shimmer of the sun upon it. Something in Cleo's eyes, something in her voice, had made fingers of apprehension tighten about Fay's heart. What did Cleo know about Lew? What was it brought that alarming expression of — of repugnance into her brown eyes? Fay shivered in the sun, aware of an urgent desire to question Cleo, an urgency that so frightened her that she abruptly leaped to her feet, holding Eric's sticky hand and running him down the beach and into the sea.

She didn't want to know! She ran swiftly from Cleo's knowledge, welcoming the clean rush of the sea. All the yesterdays when she had not known Lew didn't matter — mustn't matter: for in that direction lay heartbreak, lay the knowledge that yesterdays in his life held the girl who had won his love — and then killed it.

Fay had heard Cleo say, "Thank God for Ted!" and it was really only a matter of days after she said it that she came to Fay's apartment, breaking into a storm of tears as she threw herself down on the big white couch in the sitting room.

Fay knelt by her side in alarm. "What is it, Cleo? Has anything happened to Eric?"

"Ted wants a divorce!" Cleo gasped. "He asked me — he asked me last night. I can't believe it! I thought

41

he loved me. We've always — we've always got on so well." Cleo's sobs tore raggedly out of her throat and her small hands clenched and dragged at the scarlet cushions on the couch.

Fay watched her, aware of profound shock. Cleo had been so sure of Ted's love. She had been so certain that he would never hurt her. "Oh, Cleo," she whispered, "I am so sorry, so sorry!"

"I had no idea!" Cleo gasped. "I never dreamed he might be seeing somebody else. When he came home late, I thought he was working. I believed him when he said he was working. How could he do it? We've been married seven years. Seven years, Fay!" She sat up, pushing the dark hair back from her wet, crumpled face. "You'd think, wouldn't you, that after seven years you'd know a guy? I thought I knew Ted. I was sure I did. It just goes to show how you can be fooled; just because a guy goes on acting the same — saying the same things, laughing at the old jokes! And kissing!" Cleo's voice rose. "They're monsters! Men are monsters! They must be, to be able to do it." Her voice cracked. "How do we ever fall in love with them? What makes us?"

"Perhaps we're born fools," Fay said. Her arms encircled Cleo almost fiercely for a moment. "I don't know what to say, Cleo. Words don't really help, do they? Look, I'm going to the kitchen to make some coffee. Will you be all right?"

Cleo nodded, dabbing at her streaming eyes with a tiny scrap of lace-embroidered handkerchief. "Yes, make some coffee — I could use some coffee."

But when Fay returned with the coffee, the room was empty. Cleo had gone. The scarlet cushions on the couch were crumpled where she had lain on them in her torment, and her handkerchief lay crumpled on the floor. Fay set the coffee things on one side and stooped to pick up the handkerchief. The heliotrope

42

scent on it drifted forlornly to her nostrils. Poor Cleo! So happy yesterday, laughing in that gay little restaurant downtown, saying that Ted had been thinking lately of getting a new blue coupe.

Ted Nixon had only been thinking lately of getting a divorce!

A few days later a letter arrived from Cleo; a rather forlorn letter, which Fay read forlornly.

Cleo had left Hollywood. She and Eric had returned to her parents' home in Newport. She wanted no more of Ted, she wrote. "My love, that was so alive, is now a dead thing, Fay," she said in that letter. "But I have my little Eric; I thank God that I have my little boy....."

Fay's hands clenched on the letter and she stared beyond it to where the sunshine danced gaily on the soft gray walls of the sitting room, glittered on the pendulums of a little French clock on the bureau. The clock ticked softly and the faint hum of passing traffic came through the open window — and Fay knew that pert, gay Cleo would no longer laugh with that bubbling abandon that had been so infectious. The love she had borne Ted Nixon had been the mainspring of that wonderful laughter — but Ted Nixon had thought fit to kill that love. And Cleo had cried:

"Men are monsters!"

CHAPTER FOUR

BUT Cleo's departure from Hollywood meant that Fay was left alone again, and Lew, noticing that she seemed depressed, came home in the lunch hour one day and took her back to the studios with him.

He handed her over to a tall, boyish-looking blonde with freckles, whom he introduced as his secretary, Pat Merryweather.

"Show this baby of mine the works, Pat," he said. "Let her see the lions. She's a nice quiet kid, so hang on to her, I don't want her lost." Then he lightly touched Fay's cheek and strode off.

Pat laughed and linked her arm in Fay's. "You'd better consider yourself highly honored," she said. "Visitors aren't usually allowed. Lew's evidently been turning his celebrated charm on K. C."

"Who's K. C.?" Fay asked.

"Well, among the coast elite, of which I'm not a member, he's Karl Christbel. But among the lesser fry, of whom I am definitely numbered, he's King Christmas." Pat laughed. "He, honey, is the guy who butters your bread."

"Lew's boss?"

"Exactly."

For two hours and more, Fay wandered through this fantastic world of celluloid make-believe with the friendly Pat Merryweather. It had to be admitted that the noise and the excitement effectively stole away her depression.

She saw Shane Ardath, the biggest, latest thing in

44

screen heroes, enact a tragic scene for a new Civil War saga. She heard Silva Copperdene, a beautiful black singer from New Orleans, record a number for a big new musical. And jumping aside to avoid one of the ever-rolling trolleys of heavy scenery, she bumped smack into a stocky young man with a head of rioting black curls and a pair of laughing almond-shaped eyes. He steadied her with quick hands and laughed into her face. "My, but you're nice!" He made growling noises at her, while Pat Merryweather burst into a chuckle to see Fay's eyes fly wide with panic. Then she said to the young man, "Jerry, this is my guvnor's wife."

"Lew Marsh!" He withdrew his hands from Fay's slim shoulders in mock horror. "That guy is seven feet high, I'll depart to find me another sweet lady." His almond eyes smiled straight into Fay's. "You're sweet as a dew-drenched daisy, little one. Tell the big boy I said so — the name's Jerry Kaufmann; he'll hit the ceiling." He was gone with the words, his hands thrusting into the pockets of a noisy check jacket.

"Well!" Fay said.

"Quite!" Pat said. "Clever as a monkey, that one, but with the morals of an alley cat, I'm afraid. You'll probably see him on the set of *Corn In The City* later; he's in it. Now, how about you and me wending our thirsty way to the canteen for coffee and doughnuts?"

"I'd love to!" Fay said at once.

The canteen was fairly full and Fay gazed with wonder at the multi-costumed, heavily made-up couples and groups sitting at the tables. They didn't look at all glamorous. They looked rather bizarre, Fay thought; like people at a carnival. She said to Pat, as they sat down with their cups of coffee and their big, puffed-up doughnuts, "Some of this is rather disillusioning. These people," she gestured at the nearby tables, "look like clowns."

"Well, it's only a factory, more or less," Pat said.

"Take furniture. If you saw the nails going into it and the glue going onto it, you'd wonder how come it all looked so darned nice in the shop window. Movies are just the same." She dipped her doughnut in her coffee and ducked a hungry head to it, her white but rather widely spaced teeth snapping on the soggy doughnut with frank enjoyment.

Then her eyes, gazing over Fay's shoulder, grew suddenly narrow, and a grotesque look of exaggerated pain spread over her face. "Fried cat!" she growled. "Here comes that awful Van Deen woman!"

Thalia Van Deen! Fay bit her lip. The woman was a gossip columnist, and Fay had had the doubtful pleasure of meeting her just once at a party. She had disliked her immediately. Once, in a book she had read that the antipathy existing between some people, and which just can't be overcome, was very often due to their coloring; it produced an allergy as strong as that produced by cats, or birds, in some people. Fay believed that red-haired people did this to her, for Thalia was the third red-haired person she had met who immediately made her want to jump to her feet and run out of the room.

She had that feeling now, her hands closing tight around her coffee cup. "I thought you said visitors weren't allowed?" she said to Pat. "Isn't she a visitor?"

"She, honey, is Daddy Christmas's little ginger kitten. When Daddy feels smoochy, Thalia's there."

Fay looked rather shocked. "Is that a fact?"

Pat grinned and pressed a hand to her heart. "Scout's honor!"

Then spiky heels clicked on the floor behind them and an exotic pefume eddied to Fay's nostrils. She tensed as Thalia arrived at the table, clad in a dress that exactly matched the cat-green of her eyes, wearing a smile that was so malicious it was almost an open insult. "Why, if it isn't Lew Marsh's little bride!"

46

she gushed. "How nice to see you again!" Then she swung her green glance to Pat, airily dunking a doughnut and calmly meeting Thalia's malicious eyes. "My, no wonder you're putting on weight, Pat Merry-weather," Thalia said. "Fancy eating those nauseous things, they're just loaded with starch." She sank down gracefully in a chair facing Fay and took out her cigarette case. "I won't offer you one," she said to Fay. "They're Egyptian and horribly potent, an acquired taste, in fact." She smiled, her green eyes glinting as she put one of the slim, yellowish cigarettes into her mouth and lit it. "How are you liking Hollywood?" she asked.

"All right, thanks," Fay assured her, recoiling a lit-tle from the rank smoke of the cigarette.

"Liking married life?" Thalia pursued.

"Yes, thanks!" Fay quickly lifted her coffee cup and buried her nose in it.

Pat laughed. "The girl would be a fool if she wasn't liking married life with a guy like Lew Marsh," she remarked.

Thalia's thin lips curled. "You're always exceedingly coarse, aren't you, Pat? Is it mere affectation, or were you born like that?"

"I'm not coarse, I'm honest," Pat said, leaning back in her chair and watching Thalia with amused eyes.

Thalia shrugged, delicately, shaking ash off her cigarette. "I hate coarseness. It's a sign of pioneer blood. Have you pioneer blood, Pat?"

"It's blood, at any rate. It isn't poison," Pat replied, grinning.

Thalia stared at her, then with a smile of con-temptuous dismissal, she turned her green eyes on Fay. "Do you know," she said, softly, "you're remarkably like a friend I used to have. Her name was Inez Holden."

Pat gave a little snort and Fay glanced at her

47

enquiringly. "Never in your life is Fay like Inez!" Pat exclaimed.

"Oh, come," Thalia laughed, "there's a decided resemblance. Fay's just a little more — virginal-looking, shall I say?"

"Inez was beautiful!" Pat declared flatly. She grinned at Fay. "No offence, but Thalia's talking absolute bilge."

"Oh, I know Inez was beautiful," Thalia purred, "but Fay has her coloring. And the shape of her face is the same."

"Who was Inez Holden?" Fay asked, intrigued by their wrangling and not a bit upset that the unknown Inez should have been beautiful while she was not.

"Oh, don't you know?" Thalia exclaimed, her green eyes widening, "Hasn't Lew ever mentioned her?"

"Thalia, why don't you shut up about Inez?" Pat growled.

Thalia ignored her. She watched Fay, the rank smoke of her cigarette drifting from her thin, scarlet lips. The expression in her eyes at that moment could have been likened to the hungry, cruel look that comes into a cat's eyes just before it pounces on a mouse. "Lew was once engaged to Inez," she said, purringly. "Didn't you know? She was an actress. Not a very good one, I'll admit, but she was too beautiful for any lack of talent to really matter. She — died, you know."

"Oh Thalia, don't go raking all that up!" Pat exploded. "You're always the same, always wanting to dig up dirt."

"But, Pat dear, Fay ought to be told about Inez. I'd hate her to hear the story from people less disposed to be friendly."

"You're not disposed to be friendly," Pat retorted, flatly. "You're only out to make mischief."

Fay watched the two of them, beginning to get rather frightened. So that girl had died — that girl she

48

resembled! That girl in Lew's past! "Look," she said to Thalia, a small wash of defiant color coming into her face, "I don't want to hear anything — anything nasty about Lew, if you don't mind."

"Nasty or not, it's the truth!" Thalia flashed. "I know. I was Inez's closest friend." Suddenly she leaned across the table, staring straight into Fay's eyes. "That girl died — and Lew Marsh was as responsible for her death as if he had held a loaded revolver to her head and pulled the trigger."

Fay stared back at her, a flinching, frightened mouse before a cat, held as still in her chair as though turned to stone, her heart filled with an aching, inexplicable dread all of a sudden.

When Thalia began to speak again, the purr was gone from her voice and a shimmering spite lay in her eyes, bright green under the mass of blatant red hair. "Inez was lovely, like a tall golden flower — and then one night she ended up under the wheels of a truck, because Lew Marsh, that high and mighty swine, threw her out of his life. He said she'd played him for a sucker, but I'll never believe it. She loved him; she would have laid down on the ground and let him walk over her. She didn't deserve to be hurt as he hurt her — breaking her contract with Karl Christbel, putting it around that she was pure poison to work with. . . ." Thalia gave a thin-lipped smile at Fay's gasp of pain. "Yes, my dear, that's exactly what he did. He brazenly admitted at the inquest that he had 'shown her the door,' as he so nicely put it. He knew himself responsible for that lovely kid's death, yet he walked from that courtroom with all the urbanity in the world — he might have been walking from a restaurant. And he smiled, oh, so charmingly, for the photographers as he went out!"

Thalia sat back. She lifted her yellowish cigarette and drew on it, slowly expelling the pungent smoke.

Her eyes stared straight into Fay's. "Inez was dead — and he smiled! He smiled!"

Fay shivered, and when a warm hand touched her she glanced up to see Pat, who had risen and come round to her side. "Come on, kid," Pat said quietly, "let's get out of here."

Fay rose and without another glance at Thalia walked with Pat from the canteen. She felt dazed. Surely it couldn't be true! Lew — Lew wasn't that callous! She glanced at Pat, at her frowning, disturbed face, not half so boyish now that the wide mouth was no longer curled in a cheerful smile. "They're true, then, the things she said?" Fay spoke carefully, keeping her voice pitched to a slow deliberateness. She held no real hope that Pat would deny Thalia's story; there had been a ring of unmistakable truth in that thin voice; a gloating satisfaction in those green eyes, which no lie could have brought to them.

Pat nodded miserably. "They were engaged, and then suddenly they weren't, and Inez — Inez was out of a job. And Lew has never denied being responsible. I — I mean, if it wasn't true, he'd be bound to deny the story, wouldn't he?"

Fay's heart grew colder than ever within her, her pain sharper, her nausea stronger. As Pat said, Lew would surely have denied such a despicable story, had he been able to. That he had never done so could only mean that it was true. . . .

When they arrived on the set where Lew was working, directing a scene for *Corn In The City*, Fay stared through the cluster of tall cameras and arc lamps, seeing only the face and figure of Lew. He stood in the middle of the set, which depicted a cheap, sordid pool room, and he was arguing with a short, wiry young man. The mop of curly dark hair was all on end where his demonstrative hands had been at it, and those long, almond-shaped eyes were flashing as he argued, gesturing and gesticulating all the while, with Lew.

Fay saw only Lew, so big and vigorous, the sleeves of his shirt rolled above the elbows of his brown arms, his black hair gleaming under the powerful studio lights, and she wondered how he could look as he did, how it was possible he was so monstrous beneath those wonderful good looks. She wondered, in a dull agony, why Thalia's dreadful revelation hadn't killed her love stone dead. But it hadn't. Even as she watched Lew, she felt the familiar quick tug at her heart. A surge of almost primitive gladness that she was his swept through her — and she despised herself. She was held in thrall by him, even now, when she knew the worst of him, and she silently cried out against her own weakness.

Pat said, speaking with a forced brightness, "I told you you'd see Jerry again." A little laugh broke from her. "They're always arguing, those two. Jerry's a darn good actor, but he doesn't like being told what to do. They've been fighting over this particular scene for a couple of days now; Lew won't rest until Jerry does the scene his way and Jerry will deliberately play Lew to the verge of murder before he gives in."

"Will he give in?" Fay asked, with dull disinterest.

"Oh, he will in the end," Pat said, "because Lew happens to be right about how this scene should be played. But Jerry just likes to be difficult — with Lew, anyway."

"Another member of the fan club?" Fay enquired bitterly.

Pat stared at her. Then she looked away, saddened by the shocked despair in Fay's eyes. Poor kid! She was learning fast — along with the thrills Lew Marsh could give a woman were disillusion and heartache.

When Lew glanced up and saw Fay and Pat standing to one side of the set, he abruptly dismissed Jerry Kaufmann and came to them.

"Enjoying yourself?" He grinned down at Fay, reaching out a hand and brushing a piece of doughnut sugar from the side of her mouth.

She nodded. She even produced a smile, wondering how she could behave with this naturalness, when every shocked, aching nerve in her was crying out for expression. She longed to shed wild tears and wash the nauseated disillusion out of her system. She longed for the courage to turn and run from his callous presence.

"Noisy dump, isn't it?" Lew said, waving a big hand about, indicating the hurrying bustle everywhere. "Don't ask me how we produce order out of this chaos." He shot a grin at Pat. "I'll be spreading a little blood as well, if Kaufmann doesn't soon quit the ballerina tantrums."

Pat looked sympathetic. "Hang on, Lew, he'll come round to your way of thinking."

"He's going to have to!" Lew retorted. He turned again to Fay. "I'll be through in half-an-hour, honey, then I'll take you home — via Olive Hadley's. I want to call on her for a bit of business." His eyes held a sudden gleam, an anticipatory gleam that mingled with an amusement and an indulgence Fay was too far gone in misery to notice; or if she noticed, to wonder at.

"All right," she said.

"By the way," he said to Pat, "did you phone the Brill Agency about that singer?"

She looked disconcerted. "Oh, Lew, I forgot! I'll go and do it now." She caught hold of Fay's hand. "You come with me. You might get trampled on if you hang about here."

"I'll definitely be through in half-an-hour," Lew promised. As he strode back on to the set of *Corn In The City*, Fay turned and went with Pat to her office.

Half an hour later, Lew's car swung out of the gates of the studios and he drove rapidly in the direction of

52

Sunset Boulevard. Doing most of the talking he didn't seem to notice that Fay was extremely quiet. As they drew in before the swanky facade of Hadley House, he leaped from the car with an eager agility. "Come on," he said, holding out his hand to Fay.

"Do you need me?" she asked.

He grinned. "Not particularly, but you might as well come in, it's hot out here in the sun." He grasped her hand and drew her from the car, and he didn't release her hand as they walked in through the swing doors of Hadley House. She felt absurdly like a child.

"Lew, let me go!" she whispered, as one of Olive's elegant receptionists came across the sea-green carpet towards them. He merely laughed. He said to the girl, "It's okay, Miss Hadley's expecting us." And he swept Fay past the girl with her delicately raised eyebrows.

"You can let go of my hand," she said. "I shan't run."

"I like holding your hand." He was in a curiously light-hearted mood, his face boyish as he gazed down at her. "It's such a small, cool hand, all delicate bones. I could crush it in my paw." Then, as they stood together in that smoothly flying lift, he lifted her hand and buried his lips against her wrist.

His lips were warm, and they seemed to stay forever against the wild throb of her pulse. Fay watched his bent head. For now — for now, it pleased him to do this! Now she was his whim, his toy, but the whim would die and she would go the way of that other girl, whose name tolled in her head with a funereal insistence. She wanted to say that name, show him that she knew it — but she only mutely bore his kiss.

The lift halted and they got out. Lew, still holding Fay's hand, made straight for Olive Hadley's office. The speed of his stride made Fay glance at him, puzzled. "Your business with Olive Hadley must be important, Lew."

"My business with Olive is important." He grinned as he spoke.

CHAPTER FIVE

When Fay and Lew entered her office, Olive Hadley was behind her big desk, busily dictating to her secretary. She immediately dismissed the girl and came round the desk to them, very smart in a black suit, with a glittering diamond pin upon the lapel. She wasn't a particularly shapely or handsome woman, but the air with which she wore her superb clothes helped enormously to give her a handsome appearance. To Fay, and to dozens of other women, she always appeared the quintessence of enviable smartness and self-assurance.

"Hullo, my dear," she said to Fay. "Let me see, I've got to wish you many happy returns of the day, haven't I?"

One of Fay's hands flew to her startled mouth. Of course, she was twenty-four today — and she had forgotten! Forgotten her own birthday! "Why — why, yes," she stammered.

Lew laughed. "Go and get the coat, Olive," he said. "I can't wait to see Fay in it."

Olive went across the room to the door. She opened it and Fay heard her say to the woman at the desk outside, "Paula, run downstairs and fetch me that mink coat of Mrs. Marsh's."

Fay turned to look at Lew, who was lounging against Olive's desk, casually pressing the onyx cigarette-lighter that stood on the desk on and off. His eyes grew mocking as they surveyed her perturbed face. "You don't have to look as though I'm buying you a

54

piece of rope to strangle yourself with," he drawled.

But when the girl Paula brought the big lilac-colored box that held the coat, and Olive drew it out in all its dark, gleaming luxuriance, Fay did indeed feel as though a piece of rope had been put around her throat, choking her.

She stood very still as Lew came over to her and stood behind her, watching their reflections in the long mirror she stood in front of. She felt his hands on her shoulders, felt him smoothing the wonderful fur of the coat. His voice came softly to her ear, "Many happy returns of the day, my dear," he said.

Her eyes met his in the mirror. She felt a sensation of helplessness, of almost overwhelming weakness. She was glad of the support of his chest at the back of her, the holding of his hands. She felt certain she would have toppled to the floor without them. Today she had learned to what cruel depths he could sink — and today he made her this beautiful present. Such bitter irony moved her dangerously closer to those tears she had wanted to shed at the studios.

"Thank you for the coat, Lew," she said carefully. "It's beautiful."

But he frowned as she made her formal little "thank you" speech. He was abruptly irritated by the lack of enthusiasm in her voice, in her eyes. Couldn't she see what the coat did for her? Couldn't she see that her face nestled like a pale flower in the rich darkness of the collar? Had she no vanity, this funny kid he had plucked out of the plush stuffiness of Laurel Bay; rescued from the plaintive sickrooms of the elderly?

"I wanted to cheer you up a little," he murmured.

She turned to him then. She could see that he was disappointed in her reception of his present and she was moved to reassure him. She was genuinely touched by his realization of how upset she had been by Cleo Nixon's departure from Hollywood. "I really do like the coat, Lew." She touched tentative fingers to his sleeve. "I'm just a little bowled over, that's all."

"Of course she is," Olive Hadley broke in amusedly. "Any woman would be staggered by a coat like that, Lew." She watched them, thinking, with a rare touch of sentimentality, that they were a well-matched couple. Many people disagreed with her. They called Fay a bloodless little nonentity, but she personally considered that Lew Marsh had picked himself a winner.

There was heart and courage in the girl's face, and if that storm-tossed guy had any sense, he'd hang on to her for all he was worth. She'd give him the things he needed, the things he should have; a real home, a gentle, constant love — and children. There was no chittering, modern nonsense about Fay; she wouldn't think that providing a man with a happy home was a bore. She wouldn't put her time and preservation of her figure before a man's natural desire for children.

It was only to be hoped, for both their sakes, that Lew realized her worth. If he were only playing with her, he'd surely live to regret it!

She watched Fay as she reached out her hand and pressed Lew's arm. She wondered at the queer look of shock in her eyes. Surely being given a mink coat, even one as fabulously expensive as this, hadn't put that look in the girl's eyes?

Lew swung round to Olive. He was grinning. "She looks kind of cute, eh?" he said.

Olive nodded. "I must say Fay's air of fragility blends very well with mink. So many women merely make it look bold and expensive."

Fay colored at the compliment and when Lew turned to study her with renewed interest, his fancy caught by Olive's remark, she shrank from the admiring possessiveness suddenly very much alive in the depths of his dark eyes. She wasn't thrilled by the

56

look. She wanted, instead, to turn and flee from it.

She knew a deadly, bewildering sense of disenchantment. Lew had toppled from his mountain top. He no longer dwelt in solitary splendor in her heart. Now there stood at his side the shadowy image of that tall golden girl, who had died because she, too, had been foolish enough to love him.

She took off the coat and Olive came over and carefully replaced it in the lilac box.

"We'll christen that tonight," Lew said, wrapping a boyish arm about Fay and pulling her to his side. "I've got tickets for *A Touch of Heaven*."

"It's a great show, Lew." Olive gave him a quick smile of enthusiasm. "I saw it the other night. The music and the costumes are really something! You'll love it."

"Good!" He tipped Fay's face up to him. "That'll put a nice finish to a nice day, eh, sweetheart?"

Fay tried hard to forget what Thalia Van Deen had told her about the terrible death of Inez Holden, but she never really succeeded. Now everything seemed spoiled. When she looked at Lew across a restaurant table, watched his dark, handsome face crease in laughter or grow animated in conversation, she was no longer moved to the old spontaneous pride in his looks. She no longer thought, "This man, whom people turn to watch, is my husband."

When, at a party, he stood among a group of film people and she watched him argue, saw him impatiently flick ash off his cigar, his arrogant head thrown back, his chiselled mouth scornful, she saw him almost as a stranger.

Even when he kissed her, she was remembering. She was thinking, "Once he kissed Inez Holden. Once he held her in his arms. But he left her — and he'll leave me."

57

And in this mood of disillusionment and perplexity, she met Jerry Kaufmann again.

It was down on the beach. She still went quite often, though a little sadly, remembering the happy hours she had spent there with Cleo and Eric.

She sat thinking about Cleo and the various times she had borrowed Eric when Cleo drove to Pasadena to see an aunt. She missed taking him back to the apartment with her and feeding him melon and jelly buns, letting him thump on the piano, and lying on the carpet with him, as absorbed as he in an enormous jig-saw puzzle. Once Lew, arriving home early from work, had joined them on the carpet, a cigar clamped in his teeth as he winked his eye at Eric and carefully fitted in the pieces that formed the white kepis of a line of French Legionnaires firing upon a band of charging Arabs.

Fay sighed and ran the glistening sand through her fingers. Her melancholy eyes were fixed upon the incredibly blue sea, dotted with swimmers and surfboard riders and tall girls tossing huge rainbow balls to one another. She was not entirely unaware that on this gay stretch of beach, alive with bronzed, lounging gods and goddesses who talked and laughed, she stood out a little quaintly, even a little forlornly. She was a lone, slim figure in a lemon bathing suit that revealed only a slight bust, pale slender legs and ankles so delicately boned they looked as though they'd break if she ran too hard on them.

When a quick, amused voice said behind her, "Is it okay if I join you — you look a little in need of company?" she jumped, turning a startled face to the speaker: She recognized Jerry Kaufmann at once. His dark curls now, were wetly plastered down from the sea, and his almond-shaped eyes, surrounded by lashes as long as a girl's, were smiling.

He threw himself down beside her on the sand, stretching out his wiry, tanned body. "Boy, what a day!" he exclaimed. "If only that molten sky would open up and pour with beautiful rain!" He lounged back on his elbow, grinning sociably. "What are you doing all on your own on a Saturday afternoon?" he asked.

"I'm always on my own on a Saturday afternoon." She smiled slightly. "Lew plays golf."

"I'll remember that!" His almond eyes travelled her face, friendly and warm. "Tell me you don't mind me sitting with you."

"I don't mind." And it was true, she didn't mind. She rather liked him, she realized. Liked the sturdy, independent set to his shoulders, the frank friendliness of his eyes.

"You seemed so blue, I just couldn't resist coming over," he said. "I always think that being alone on a beach is the next worse thing to being alone at a hotdog stand." He grinned. He had a very engaging grin, showing small, square teeth. "Hollywood can be a very lonely place for a stranger." He spoke sympathetically.

"It reminds me of a jungle," she said, moved to impulsive frankness by the friendly way in which he was regarding her. Though he was a perfect stranger, he didn't seem like one. He had a naturalness of manner that set her quite at ease, an open, confident glance that won her confidence without any effort. "It's so hot and sultry; full of strange noises and handsome, dangerous creatures who pounce." She smiled. "I know that I'm silly to let it scare me, but it does scare me."

"You've no mad ambitions to break into movies, then?" he asked.

She shook her head, her dimples arriving in her cheeks to give her a roguish look that Jerry Kaufmann found very alluring. "Lew would probably toss me out of the sitting room window if ever I developed the fever to be a film star," she said.

59

Jerry grinned. "That would be a pretty drastic remedy. Why would he do that, do you suppose?" He watched her, studying her delicately curving cheekbones, her mouth like a flower, her throat that was as sweetly hollowed as a child's.

"Why, I'd develop a temperament to match my mad ambitions, wouldn't I?" she said. "Lew prefers me without one. He says he gets his share of temperament all day long at the studios. Anyway, I'm not the film star type."

"That's true," Jerry agreed. "You strike me as — as retiring, shall I say?"

"You don't mean placid and mediocre, do you?" Her smile was rueful. She had, in these weeks in Hollywood, grown to think of herself in those terms. Everyone here seemed possessed of enormous talent, or tremendous vitality, or extraordinary good looks. People still gaped when they saw her with Lew and were told she was his wife, and Fay was slowly but surely learning to be blasé about the incredulity of these people.

"I think," Jerry Kaufmann said, with a flattering promptness, "that you're a very refreshing change from the overflow of lush opulence that one sees around here at every turn of the head. You're as cool as rain."

As cool as rain, he thought, and sweet as a spray of mimosa. A gentle, timid kid who stirred an unexpected protectiveness in him. Who stirred, as well, a kind of shocked recoil when he thought of her imprisoned in the powerful arms of Lew Marsh, at the mercy of that hard, insolent mouth. To escape the thought, he said to her, "Do you swim?"

"Not very professionally," she admitted. She knew, just by looking at him, that he'd be superbly proficient in the water. He had the tough, well knit body of the good swimmer, and when he leaped to his feet, pulling her up with him, he moved with the easy grace of a dancer.

"Let's go swim," he suggested. "This sand is as hot as a grill." He held her hand and ran her down the beach and into the sea, laughing with the mad abandon of a boy, his wet curls flopping on to his forehead.

That night, over dinner, Fay told Lew that she had spent the afternoon swimming with Jerry Kaufmann. She was curious to see how he reacted to the information, sensing that he disliked Jerry, but she was unprepared for the quick flash of anger that came into his eyes.

"The devil you did!" he exclaimed. "I suppose the little swine was very chummy?"

Fay, in her turn, grew rather angry. "That isn't a very nice way to talk about him," she said. "I thought he was quite nice."

"Kaufmann!" Lew laughed. "I could tell you things about that guy that would make that pretty gold hair of yours stand on end. You'll stay away from him, if you don't mind." He looked straight into her eyes. "I'm not merely asking you to, Fay, I'm telling you to."

She was taken aback by his tone. She stared at him, half expecting him to break into a smile and reveal that he was joking with her, but when he didn't, she grew defiant. "You could tell me to go jump out of a window, but that doesn't mean I'm obliged to do it," she retorted, rather childishly.

His eyes narrowed as he looked at her across the table. "As it happens, my baby, where Kaufmann's concerned, you'd do better to jump out of a window. It's quicker that way."

"Quicker?" She didn't understand him.

"I'm implying that Kaufmann's sheer murder." He poured himself a glass of wine and he grinned at her over the rim as he lifted the glass to his lips. "What are you thinking: that I'm no spotless angel myself? Now that strikes me as a little sad. You used to hold such touching optimistic views about me, Fay. What's happened to them lately?"

She looked across at his dark, quizzical face. He was sipping his wine, his eyes mocking her. "I don't think I really care any more whether you're capable or incapable of improvement," she told him. "You're what you are, aren't you? I accept you for what you are."

He raised a black brow at her. "That's a somewhat ambiguous remark, my pet," he drawled. "Would you mind amplifying it a little?"

"Tigers don't change their stripes, do they?" Her soft mouth twisted. "I was under the delusion that they did, that's all."

"I see." He studied her, her set face and her rather defiant eyes. "What's gone wrong, Fay?" he asked, quietly. "What have I done?"

And something in the way he said those few quiet words got right under Fay's guard, sent such a thrill of pain through her that she gave a little gasp.

"Don't take any notice of me," she murmured. "I'm a fool, that's all."

His brows climbed quizzically. "Why, because you thought you could cover up the tiger's stripes with a handful or two of whitewash?" He smiled and twirled his wine glass, watching the golden sparkle of the wine through the glass. "I see that you've found out it would take rather more than that to hide my stripes. I'm sorry the discovery has hurt you, Fay."

He lifted his glass with a cynical flourish and drained it, his eyes intent on Fay's face; slanting, quizzical eyes, still capable of melting her knees and filling her arms with a queer, aching longing to hold him. Then he gave a short laugh and rose to his feet. "Come and dance," he said. "You forget to think up questions about me when I've got you close to me."

CHAPTER SIX

FAY tried, after that conversation, to do as Lew wished; she tried to keep away from Jerry, but it suddenly seemed that everywhere she went, Jerry was there. If she went down to the beach, he joined her. If she went to the park to listen to the band, sooner or later he came hanging over the back of her seat, thrusting popcorn under her nose.

And at parties, when Lew disappeared to play poker or to talk films, Jerry would inevitably appear at her side, drinks in his hands or an invitation to dance on his lips.

He was always so friendly and casual and entertaining that Fay was at a loss to understand why Lew had spoken as he had about him. No one, she thought, could have treated her with more respect than Jerry did. Even when they danced he didn't hold her too close to him, as did some of the other men who frequented these parties. He never attempted the shadow of a familiarity.

She began to think that Lew had let the fact that he and Jerry couldn't work properly together distort his judgment, his sense of fairness. Jerry, she decided, was a lot less harmful than Lew was himself, and though the acknowledgment filled her with a painful sense of disloyalty, she held to it. She used it as her excuse to forget, even to dismiss, Lew's injunction that she keep away from Jerry.

She definitely liked him. She never openly encouraged him, but she knew that the pleasure she felt in his company must show in her eyes when they laughed together over some inane joke that he somehow turned into a witticism. Or when they made a thorough mess of surf-board riding. Or when they stood together at a hot-dog stand and he plied her with the peppery things, trying to make her as enthusiastic about them as he was himself.

He had, Fay realized, taken Cleo Nixon's place in her new life; he had become the friend she needed so badly. She accepted him, wholeheartedly, as a friend. It never once occurred to her that he could ever mean, or ever want to mean, anything more than that to her. She never even noticed that in his own zestful, gamin way, he was very attractive; nor was she particularly impressed by the fact that he was one of the most popular young actors in Hollywood. To her, he was just Jerry — Jerry of the boyish grin, the irrepressible spirit. She was so busy being grateful for his friendship that she didn't notice the amused, speculative glances they were beginning to attract at parties.

One Saturday afternoon he took her to a ball game. She had never been before, and though it was all a bit of a mystery to her, she was soon cheering as enthusiastically as Jerry. And it was in the midst of her cheering that the toffee apple Jerry had bought her flew off the end of its stick and landed a couple of rows down, plunking stickily into the ample lap of a rather glum-faced supporter of the visiting team.

When the indignant head swivelled to find the culprit, Fay was obligingly obeying Jerry's swiftly whispered and barely understandable injunction — she was trying so desperately hard not to burst out laughing — to look as though butter wouldn't melt in her mouth.

The poor man, so unjustifiably bombarded with the enormous and revoltingly sticky toffee apple, met big blue eyes so unutterably innocent, so overwhelmingly devoid of anything approaching guilt or the juvenile desire for such a ridiculous thing as a toffee apple, that any consequences, in the form of glum vituperation from this glum-faced victim of so messy an assault, passed Fay by. The glaring, offended eyes searched the row and Fay could feel the shaking of Jerry's body as he fought to control his laughter. "Stop it!" she whispered. "He'll guess in a minute if you go much redder in the face."

"How — how do you do it?" Jerry gasped. "You look too darn angelic for words. He's looking at you again!" In a sudden excess of uncontrollable hysteria, Jerry bent as though to fasten his shoe and Fay could hear him sniggering and hoarsely gulping down by her knee. It was all she could do to keep a straight face herself.

She enjoyed that ball game as she hadn't enjoyed anything for a long time, and when they finally drifted out with the bemused and noisy crowd and Jerry casually said to her, "If you've time, how about coming back to my place for a coke or coffee?" she agreed, almost eagerly.

She had never been to Jerry's apartment before and she was astounded by the prevailing untidiness of the place, it's Bohemian atmosphere of chaotic indiscrimination. This sitting room, with its conglomeration of bizarre furniture and its big windows looking out over the sea, was more like a studio than anything else. Especially so since a covered easel stood by one of the windows, in such a position as to catch the streaming light.

"Do you paint, Jerry?" she asked, eyeing the easel with frank curiosity.

He shrugged, grinning at her. "Let's just say I try." He walked to the easel and flicked off the cover. "Want to examine the body?" he queried diffidently.

65

She went over to him and stood at his side. Her eyes grew very big as she discovered herself — it was herself and yet it was also someone she had never been.

She sat on a white wall, down which trailed a mass of magenta and gold flowers. Her right hand rested in the flowers, while her feet were bare as they dangled against the wall. Her head was thrown back in light and irresponsible laughter.

"Well?" Jerry asked quietly.

"It's me — yet —" she turned her wondering eyes to his face — "yet not me at all."

"Perhaps it's you as I see you — or would like to see you," he said.

"A sort of — gypsy!" she gasped incredulously. She turned again to the painting. The colors were bold and applied with a bold hand. Jerry had ripened the color of her hair, made her mouth more daring. Around her left ankle there glinted a slender bracelet, but her left hand was without its wedding ring. She hardly realized the significance of that rejected ring, so taken was she with the painting as a whole. For an amateur painting it was extremely well done. She recognized that though she knew very little about painting. Her pose was relaxed and as warmly appreciative of the sun as a kitten on a wall.

"The eyes aren't quite right," Jerry said, peering into the painted face. "I rather thought they weren't, and now that you're here I can see where I've gone wrong. Your eyes crinkle when you laugh, but they still stay big." He turned to her, looking eager. "If I bribe you with a long, cool coke, will you sit for me for fifteen minutes or so while I put those eyes in order?"

She laughed, going a little pink. "Keep it to fifteen minutes, then, Jerry," she begged. "Lew is taking me to meet his boss tonight and I daren't be late home."

"K. C.!" Jerry whistled. "Are you really going to his house?"

She nodded. "To dinner. Is he — is he very formidable, Jerry?"

Jerry grinned as he walked off to the kitchen to fetch her the promised coke. "He's absolutely indescribable!" he called back over his shoulder. "I wonder if our green-eyed friend Thalia will be there."

"Under the same roof as his wife?" Fay gasped.

She heard Jerry laugh. When he returned with two tall glasses of coke, he said, handing her one of the glasses, "K. C. is such a potentate that even his missus daren't get annoyed if he brings his mistress to dinner. The missus will surprise you. She's a magnificent, synthetic blonde of about fifty. She weighs a good 160 pounds and she adores her delinquent slob of a husband. Why he bothers with a shrill little beast like Thalia when he has a wife like Magda is a mystery to me."

"Magda?" Fay queried. "She sounds foreign."

Jerry nodded. "She's something Balkan, I think. They both are — I think." He chuckled. "Everything connected with K. C. is a bit of a mystery. Some of the things he says will set you wildly running around for a key to their meaning. He talks real jumble, and if you haven't known him half a dozen years, you'll wonder what the heck he's getting at."

Fay looked a trifle worried. "I dare say I'll go and give him a silly answer." She smiled. "I guarantee I'll tread on Lew's toes before the evening's out."

It was half-past six by the time Fay got home. Lew, hearing her come in, put his head round the bathroom door and demanded to know where she had been. "You're devilishly late, y'know," he grunted.

She nervously shed her coat. "I — I went to a movie," she blurted out, keeping her head turned from him so that he shouldn't see by her heightened color that she lied to him. "A re-issue of an old Bette Davis film was showing at the Columbia, so I went. You know I can't resist her. I always watch her movies."

"Well, buck yourself up," Lew urged. "We're due at the Christbel's by seven-thirty." The bathroom door shut and Fay stood staring rather wildly into the dressing-table mirror. This wasn't the first time she had lied to Lew. As she saw more and more of Jerry, her lies to Lew increased in number. She dreaded what would happen when he found out, but she clung determinedly to her friendship with Jerry. Why shouldn't she have him for a friend? He was a real relief to be with, a wholly charming and relaxing person. He provided relaxation for her, stirred into life the irresponsible urge to return to childhood, but to a childhood far more colorful than the reality had been.

When Lew came from the bathroom, vigorously rubbing his wet head with a towel, he gave her a quick, rather irritated glance. "Jump to it, honey, I've run your water. We haven't a lot of time, y'know. I put in two handfuls of those lavender crystals, that enough?"

She was obliged to smile. "From the size of your hands, rather more than enough, I'd say." As she passed him, she put out her own hand and drew her fingertips across his bare back. When he was like this, so boyishly fresh and clean from his bath, his brown skin gleaming, the muscles of his back and his arms rippling with health, he seemed incapable of any despicableness. He seemed like a brown god, come up out of some deep, clean pool of enchantment. He shone with a cleanliness that seemed of the spirit as well as of the body. She could almost believe in such moments that whatever evil things were said of him, they had their foundation only in the minds of the people who said them. It seemed a blasphemy to believe that he had viciously ruined a beautiful girl.

He was dressed long before she was, impatiently prompting her, as she stepped into her dress, to get a move on. "Well, come and zip me up, then," she im-

plored, looking and feeling somewhat flustered, her
hand groping impotently about behind her for the zip.
She was still uncertain whether or not she liked this
dress. Lew had wanted something special for her, this
being her first visit to the Christbels', and he had told
Olive Hadley to dream up something out of the ordinary, something capable of being worn only by Fay.
Fay secretly thought that she was the last person on
earth who should be wearing it.

It was a pure silk, extremely close fitting to the hips
and a most delicately lovely shade of lilac. From the
hips the lilac color deepened and the skirt became full,
cascading with tier upon tier of innumerable petals,
edged with tiny, glittering beads. It was a curious and
undeniably attractive mixture of innocence and stylish
originality, but Fay, gazing at herself in the mirror,
knew again that definite distaste the dress had
aroused in her when Olive had first fitted it on her.

She felt Lew's hand on the zip and when she saw the
lilac silk close like a sheath on her body, she turned
from the mirror with a quick, embarrassed gasp.

"What's the matter?" Lew caught and held her
elbows, his eyes searching hers enquiringly.

"I — I feel naked!" she gasped.

He laughed, his brows lifting in quizzing incredulity.
He stood back to examine her in the dress, slowly and
pleasurably moving his eyes over her. "You look a picture!" he declared, with emphasis. "You look like pale
innocence gone on the rampage. I told Olive nothing
'sweet young miss' and she's come up with a winner.
You'll turn a few heads tonight, my pet." He drew her
towards him, his big, shapely hands moving caress-
ingly up her sides, but she held herself rigidly back
from him, turning her head, shyness storming in her,
distressing her. Why must Lew always show so plainly
that it was her body he liked?

"Don't kiss me!" she said. "You'll — you'll spoil my

69

lipstick." She wondered if he noticed her distress.

"I might, at that," he agreed, grinning and releasing her. He turned from her and walked out to the sitting room, and Fay eyed herself without pleasure in the mirror. She took up a powder puff and lightly touched it to her nose, a reluctant smile coming to claim her mouth. Should she paint her eyes to match this actressy dress? Go all out? Make a real job of impressing the Christbels? It was perfectly obvious that Lew intended she should impress them.

With abrupt decision and a fighting angle to her chin, Fay sat down on the dressing-table stool and opened the big makeup box Lew had given her and which she so rarely used. She took out mascara and lavender eye shadow. With care, and something of defiance, she made up her eyes, watching the bewitching sparkle the coloring brought to them with an ironical expression of amusement.

When Lew came back into the room, she swung round on the stool and smilingly batted her lashes at him. She waited for the verdict as he came across the room and stood looking down at her.

"I've added a little to the rampage, Lew," she said, lightly.

"So I see. Do you feel somewhat less naked now?" He grinned wickedly as he spoke.

She nodded.

Still grinning, he raised her from the stool, turned her so that she stood with her back to him and lightly clipped a slim necklace of diamonds about her throat. The necklace clung against the white skin of her throat, throwing out small fiery flashes as he turned her again and carefully added matching diamond drops to the tiny lobes of her ears.

Her eyes, a deeper blue than ever with their lids feathered with eye shadow and their lashes darkened with mascara, stared up into his dark, smiling eyes.

"Why are you always giving me presents?" she asked, her voice tremulous all of a sudden. "You don't have to, Lew. I don't want presents all the time."

He gently touched her cheek with his finger. "Maybe that's the reason I give them to you," he replied whimsically. He went across to the big wardrobe and drew out her mink coat. As he helped her on with it, he held the big collar up about her face, studying her.

"Do I look — expensive enough, Lew?" she enquired.

"Expensive?" He shook his head. "Rather more than that, but the exact description eludes me."

"Does it, Lew?" She stood quietly between his hands, the diamonds he had given her sparkling in her ears, a smile that was just a little sad playing about her lovely mouth. "How about decorated goose, all ready for serving up on a platter to the Christbels?" she asked.

He put back his head and laughed. "You'll do!" he exclaimed. "Come on, sweetheart, let's go. K. C. has a bit of a complex about punctuality."

But they were doomed to be late at that dinner party. On the way to the Christbel's, not far from Crystal Court, the car ran out of gas and Lew had to turn in at a station to get some.

They had been here before and while Lew beckoned an attendant and had the tank refilled, Fay gazed around for the big, shaggy dog that roamed this place and which she was in the habit of petting. When she saw him appear in the doorway of the house adjoining the gas station, she gave a little whistle to attract his attention. His ears cocked in instant recognition, but as he bounded down the wooden steps of the house and darted across to greet her, a great salmon-pink car swept into the gas station and Fay's exclamation of horror mingled with the dog's shrill scream of pain.

The wheels of the pink car had smacked into him and thrown him along the gravelled front of the gas station.

Fay was gone from Lew's side in a flash. She ran to the whimpering dog, knelt down beside him and took the shaggy head upon her knee, uncaring of the blood that stained the lilac skirt of her dress and the side of her mink coat. But Lew had quickly followed and he bent above her, holding her shoulder. "Watch yourself, Fay!" He spoke urgently. "If you touch him where's he's hurt, he'll turn on you."

She ignored him, jerking her shoulder free of his fingers. She bent more closely over the dog, tears starting to her eyes at its pain and bewilderment.

But Lew's hands came relentlessly, lifting her away from the dog, and though she struggled and fought him, he determinedly set her on one side. "Stand there and keep quiet!" he ordered. "If you interfere, I'll slap you!"

He crouched down by the dog and Fay watched him pass his strong brown hands along the shaggy back of the animal. Careful as Lew was, its teeth became bared as it sought to turn and bite the hand that touched him.

Lew glanced up at the man and woman who now stood beside Fay. The woman had run out from the house and she stood with rolled sleeves, wiping wet hands on her apron, her face pale and alarmed in the glaring light. "Is he bad? Is he bad?" she demanded, while the man, presumably her husband, closed rather oily fingers about her arm. Lew nodded in answer to the question. "The poor brute should be finished," he said.

The woman cried out protestingly and her husband turned to her, speaking in a low, flurried voice: "He's right, Gert, can't you see?" He turned again to Lew. "Shall I go and get something —"

Lew shook his head. He bent over the dog and Fay clasped her silently moving mouth, while she shuddered, violently, at the single sharp blow. Lew rose slowly to his great height.

Fay backed from him, backed into the small group of people who had gathered. She stared at them, her eyes suddenly swimming in tears. "I'm sorry — I'm sorry!" she gasped, hardly knowing what she did say, only aware that she had whistled the lovable old dog under the wheels of the pink car and that Lew had been the final impassive instrument of quick death.

She turned blindly from the group of gaping people and fled across the gravel to the street.

CHAPTER SEVEN

As Fay fled, she stumbled in her flimsy high-heeled shoes, the long, blood-stained skirts of her dress held in her hands. She was almost desperate with the need to escape the sight of Lew's hands, curved to destroy — but as she reached the street, he caught her, spinning her toward him like a doll. "Where do you think you're going, you hysterical little fool?" he demanded.

She struggled fiercely, hating him; hating his insensitiveness, his ability to kill a dog with a face devoid of emotion. Hating his killing hands upon her.

"Listen," he said curtly. "That poor tyke was finished, even a vet couldn't have helped it. I did what had to be done, and the sooner you realize it and stop behaving like a melodramatic schoolgirl, the better I'll like it. Now buck yourself up. We'll be late at the Christbels'."

"The Christbels!" Abruptly she stopped struggling, staring up into his irritated face. "But I don't want to go! Not now! Not now!"

He shook her, impatiently. "You try me to the point of sheer murder at times, Fay!" He turned her and forcibly walked her to the car, uncaring that she stumbled in her high heels.

"I'm — all over blood!" she gasped. "The poor thing bled all over me!" When they reached the car, she stood by the headlights and despairingly showed him the skirt of her dress, splashed with blood and dirtied where she had knelt in oil-stained gravel.

Lew's face was expressive of various emotions in

that moment; patience tried to breaking point, annoyance as with a vexatious child, and something also of reluctant sympathy. "Now we'll have to go home and get you a change of finery. Come on, get in." He helped her into the car and she watched him with big, scared eyes as he walked round the car and climbed in beside her, slamming the door. He swung the car out of the gas station, past the group of people bent above the dead body of the dog. The forlorn sound of a woman's sobbing followed the car into the main road.

Back at the apartment, Fay followed Lew drearily into the sitting room and uttered no protest when he poured neat whiskey into a glass and made her drink it. She coughed as the spirit bit into her throat and brought tears to her eyes.

"Don't make me go with you!" She clung to his arm, lifting imploring eyes to his face. "Please Lew! It won't matter if I don't go."

"Won't it?" His mouth thinned obstinately. "I beg to differ. Come on, let's get you out of that dress."

He marched her into the bedroom, drew off her coat and carelessly tossed it to a chair, where its stained splendor slid slowly to the floor and lay forgotten on the carpet.

"Get that dress off," Lew said curtly, striding to the wardrobe and jerking open the door. He ran an impatient hand along the rack inside, pulling out a turquoise blue creation with a pattern of rose-pink sequins spreading on one side of the skirt. It was quite pretty, but nothing near as daring and flattering as the lilac dress. There was a rather dry twist to Lew's mouth as he brought the dress to Fay.

He carefully helped her into it, but he obdurately ignored her pleading eyes.

"K. C. isn't a guy who extends invitations to dinner every night of the week," he said firmly, "and I'm darned if I'll turn up there tonight without you. He

75

and Magda want to meet you and they're going to meet you. Now wipe that damned paint off your eyes, it's running. And stop looking at me as though I've committed a murder."

The house was like something out of a Civil War saga; white and graceful, with Corinthian pillars and a silver-haired black butler.

He ushered Fay and Lew into a hall of magnificent proportions, tiled in black and white, with a goldfish pond as its centerpiece and diamond-bright chandeliers flashing high in the painted ceiling. Fay felt as though she had stepped into an extravagant film set, and her very first glimpse of Karl Christbel did nothing to dispel the feeling.

Her apprehension and her nervousness, because she and Lew were late getting to the house, diminished rapidly as she was introduced to this bouncing ball of a man, all glistening bald head, glistening cheeks, and glistening black eyes. He gabbled some form of greeting at Fay, then he bounced away to the edge of the goldfish pond, where he stood scattering goldfish food into the translucent water. He looked neither the supreme power behind the great sprawling studios where Lew worked nor the amatory partner of Thalia Van Deen.

But his wife, Magda, lived up to Jerry's description of her as a magnificent heavyweight blonde in her early fifties.

She wore beautifully draped black and her many diamonds sparkled in the synthetic waves of her hair and halfway up her dimpled arms. She laughingly dismissed their latenss, saying to Lew, in a loud, accented voice, "Better late than not come at all, huh?" She turned her laughing, richly tinted face to Fay. "How come this big, bad boy bring you so late?" She reached out a plump, heavily-ringed hand and pinched

Fay's pale cheek. "Was busy kissing you, maybe?" Fay blushed and Magda gave Lew a broad wink. "Is so, huh?" Her expansive bosom shook with appreciative amusement. "Ah, well, youth is but a small time. It quickly pass. One day," she inclined her head toward Fay and swept a glittering hand down her own stout body, "one day she will look like me, then what you do, you big, bad boy?"

Lew laughed and lifted his brows at Fay, slender Fay, with her wisp of a waist and her delicate wrists and ankles. "What do you think I'll do?" he enquired of her.

She met his amused glance and she was perversely moved to retort, "I think, by that time, you'd have long since found yourself a new toy."

She turned, then, to follow Magda to the drawing room, where about eight or nine people were gathered, drinking highballs and awaiting the dinner gong. Fay was relieved to find that the dinner party was such a comparatively small one and that it did not include Thalia Van Deen.

Dinner turned out to be a long and very conversational affair; the dishes lavish and Continental, the choice of accompanying wines equally lavish.

Fay's table companions were a tall, auburn-haired girl, who appeared to be at the party on her own, and a rather cheerful man in a tartan dinner jacket, who would keep talking about his gastric ulcer, informing Fay that this dinner (which he was putting away with the gusto of a boiler attendant) would just about kill him in the morning. Fay, drawing upon her nursing experience, had to smile and agree with him.

Suddenly the girl on her left leaned toward her and said, "We're in for a bit of fun after dinner. Magda and Karl have got hold of a real live gypsy fortune teller, and according to the grapevine, we're all going to have our fortunes told." Her smile flashed gaily. "I'm hoping she's going to promise me a present like that one across the table — that big guy, talking to Magda."

Fay followed her glance across the table and a quick smile moved on her mouth as she bent her head to her duck in aspic. "That guy," the redhead continued, "gives me prickles up my spine."

"Really?" A twinkle was in Fay's blue eyes.

"Don't tell me he leaves you cold!" the girl exclaimed, looking incredulous.

"Oh, I quite agree that he's good-looking," Fay smiled.

"He's more than that!" The girl was frankly admiring Lew. "That barbaric hunk is born out of his century. I see him striding the deck of a pirate galleon, a bloodstained cutlass in his hand."

"Or racing chariots down the Appian Way," Fay murmured.

The girl's eyes sparkled into Fay's. "So you do see what I mean? You do see that touch of the brute patrician? That guy could hurt like hell, but boy, I don't think I'd mind!"

"Wouldn't you?" Fay looked curious. "Just because he's something out of the ordinary, does that mean he has to be excused an ordinary code of behavior?"

The girl considered the question, her attention caught by Fay's sudden look of seriousness. "I guess nine women out of ten would excuse that guy quite a lot. The tenth, in my opinion, would have to be a pretty cold potato." She grinned. "Don't tell me you wouldn't make excuses for that handsome brute?"

"I make them all day long." Fay's lashes swept down over her eyes. 'He's my husband."

"Wow!" The girl's fork clattered against her plate. "Wow to that! And you let me pour out my girlish, pounding heart." She laughed, shaking her auburn head. "Still, I guess you're well used to listening to the envious sighs of other women, aren't you?"

"Mostly it's their incredulous gasps I listen to," Fay returned.

The girl looked perplexed for a moment, her eyes wandering the pale earnestness of Fay's small face. Then her good-humored mouth quirked. "I'm not incredulous," she said. "I'm thinking that you're exactly the sort of kitten that big bold pirate would carry about with him. I envy you no end."

"Really?" Fay's smile held irony. Such a remark would once have pleased her, now it only seemed to her to underline Lew's mere possession of her. His kitten! His toy! His small piece of plunder!

After dinner, when they were all assembled in the handsome drawing room, Karl Christbel announced his intention of producing the fortune teller. Lew looked frankly unimpressed, calling out to Magda, "The last time I was here you sprang a bubble dancer for our edification. I had high hopes of a repeat performance, Magda. That lady was none too dexterous with those balloons."

There was a general spurt of laughter, but Magda shook a reproving head at him. "You are one bad boy, Lew," she told him. "You will have your fortune told and like it."

He turned to Fay, on the arm of whose chair he was lounging. He lazily ran his finger down her arm. "This is my fortune, Magda," he said. He grinned at Fay. "You are, aren't you, sweetheart?"

She met his eyes, sustained their dark, smiling ownership. "If you say so, Lew," she replied.

The Christbels' fortune teller was an awesome-looking creature, tall, cavernous and middle-aged, with glittering, jet-black eyes and a swarthy skin. Her left cheek carried a small tattoo and she wore any amount of cascading coins about her neck and a red bandana about her head. Her hands were large and extremely weathered. As she sat at the table to which

79

Karl Christbel conducted her she shuffled a pack of dog-earëd cards in them. Most of the assembled party were looking rather awestruck by her, but Lew was openly grinning and sweeping her gaunt figure with insolent, quizzing eyes.

She sat watching the cards as they ran through her fingers, then abruptly she glanced up and her jet eyes settled on Lew. His open amusement, his sad lack of proper regard for the art as old as the Romany race itself, had piqued the fortune teller's pride, and she singled him out, made of him her first victim.

She threw out a sudden gaunt hand toward him and her deep, harsh voice rang through the room. "You doubt my ability to read the future, don't you, young man? You think that it lies hidden behind a veil too thick for human eyes to penetrate?"

He nodded, his eyes dancing with wicked glee. "You mystification quacks don't impress me one little bit," he replied.

"You won't, then, step to this table and choose two of my cards?" she asked.

"I'll do it, for the fun of the thing." He rose from the arm of Fay's chair and approached the table. The gypsy sat moving her well-worn cards about the table top, the coins about her neck giving out a low jangling. The look she wore as she watched Lew, tall and unimpressed by her, a cigar smoking in his mouth, was wholly malignant. Then, as he drew nearer to her, a curious spasm passed over her face; her top lip seemed to lift away from her teeth and a peering, piercing look came into her eyes. Only for a second was that look distinguishable, then her black lashes swept down, veiling it.

When Lew reached the table, she gestured to him to turn two of the cards and he carelessly did so. A black king and a red joker lay side by side.

"Well," Lew drawled, "penetrate the veil, reveal the

future, if you can." Lew's challenge had a sarcastic note.

The woman began to laugh a deep, cavernous laugh that again set her yards of strung coins jangling. With a forefinger set with a hard, long nail she moved the red joker on to the black king. She said, through her laughter, "In your case, young man, it is better that I leave the veil undisturbed." Her glance went across the room to Fay, who was watching the scene at the table with large, wondering eyes. The forefinger was pointed at Fay. "For your sake I'll do this," she cried.

Lew's hand reached for the woman's shoulder, closing hard on the bony strength of it, closing until her swarthy head swivelled to him once more. "Don't try to frighten her!" he said, his voice suddenly empty of all amusement.

A curious silence lay over the room as he said that; a watching, bated silence. All eyes were upon him and the gypsy, yet Fay received the strangest impression that all thought was suddenly concentrated upon her. She shrank in her chair and prayed for an end to that scene at the table.

"It doesn't lie in my power to frighten your wife," the gypsy said, and her beak of a nose was imperious as she stared up at Lew. "It lies with you."

Then she jerked her shoulder free of his fingers and snatched up her strewn cards. She began to re-shuffle them, running her eyes round the room. "Who will come now?" she demanded, and Fay saw the auburn-haired girl who had been her companion at dinner rise and stroll to the table.

Fay was very quiet going home in the car. It had been a strange, nightmarish evening and now she felt drained of vitality, emptied of everything but a weary apprehension. She lay with her face turned from Lew, watching the darkened avenues skim by, the odor of oranges over high, white walls coming to her.

81

What had the gypsy meant? What lay in the future? Fay shivered and turned her cold cheek against the cold leather of the car. She was suddenly very close to tears, her heart crying out for reassurance, the reassurance that was not available. Her life with Lew stood on shifting sand; any day he might grow weary of her, and though she knew his cruel streak, his untamable arrogance, she shrank from a future empty of him. He might not possess the gentle understanding Jerry gave so unstintingly, but he held her heart — held, too, the power to break it.

CHAPTER EIGHT

FAY clung to her friendship with Jerry, clutching to it as though to a lifeline, feeling sometimes that if it slipped from her she would be irretrievably drowned and lost in this strange, bewildering world she had entered out of love for a man who didn't love her.

But in her innocence she didn't know that people were beginning to talk . . . which talk suddenly reached Lew's ears at a party of Olive Hadley's.

Jerry had danced Fay out onto the terrace of Olive's penthouse and as they stood looking at the fairyland of lights below them, he said, "What a night for a drive! How about it, Fay?"

"Oh, I couldn't!" she said, but her eyes, meeting his, were openly wistful. The party was smoky and noisy and the thought of a drive on such a clear, still night was infinitely tempting.

"Lew won't miss you," Jerry pressed. "He's too busy playing poker."

"How — how long would we be gone?" She was rapidly weakening and she knew it.

"Half an hour, no more." He grinned. "Come on, be a little unwifely for once. You're the talk of the town already with your devotion."

"You mean — people laugh because I sit in a corner while Lew goes off to talk films or play poker?" she said, her face going pink.

Jerry didn't deny her assertion. "I guess they do," he replied.

So Fay went with him. But they were gone a lot

longer than half an hour, Jerry's beautiful cream Cadillac ate up the miles so smoothly, so pleasantly, and it was such sheer joy to ride through the soft night, under the enormous stars, that Fay just didn't notice the passage of time.

They took the ocean road and the wind carried with it the salt tang of the sea, while the mysticism of the · moon rode high and white above the flowing black sheet of the sea. The radio in the car played softly, dreamily, and Fay gazed up at the stars, flashing points of light in midnight blue velvet — a mysterious world of singing silence flooded her with a cool release from care as she rode beside Jerry.

"Loosen your hair, Fay," he suddenly said. "Let the wind blow through it."

"Shall I?" Her eyes were big on his face. Then, with a laugh, she complied, pulling the jewelled pins from the chignon she wore tonight and dropping them into her bag.

The needle on the speedometer moved forward as Jerry pressed on the accelerator and the soft wind whipped Fay's cheeks and sent her fair hair flowing back from her face. "This is lovely!" she cried. "This is like being in a chariot, flying through the sky."

"Funny kid!" Jerry muttered, and Fay didn't notice that the usual merry twinkle was missing from his eyes. She didn't even question his unusual silence when he stopped the car upon a hill and lay back against the leather of the car, the smoke of his cigarette drifting in a thin blue line to the sky. She was content to be as silent as he, wrapped in the sure warmth of his friendship.

Then, after a while, he began to speak — to speak about himself, which was also unusual for Jerry. "Ever heard of the Bronx, Fay?" he queried.

"Vaguely," she admitted. "By way of books and some films."

"Sure." He grinned slightly. "The Bronx is notoriously fascinating to the author and the film-maker — only I lived there and I didn't find it fascinating. My folks died when I was a kid and I knocked around after that on the edge of a sprawling Jewish family. They weren't bad, but they didn't have much, they couldn't really afford to feed me, so I quit the Bronx when I was thirteen. I hitched out here to California and got me a job on a fruit farm. Then the farm folded and I got me a job mopping floors and serving beers in a pool-room — and that's how it went on, a succession of cheap jobs, too many cheap meals, and my envious eyes following the flashy, expensive cars of the movie stars day in and day out. Why not me? I thought. I had curls, I had muscles, so why not me?" He fell silent for a moment, studying the red end of his cigarette. Then he went on: "I got to be a movie star and I got this car — but sometimes I think I've got nothing. I'm thirty-two, Fay. I'm the kind of a guy who should be settled in a comfortable rut with a wife and a couple of noisy kids, but I've got nothing."

"Haven't you ever been in love, Jerry?" Fay asked quietly.

"Yeah!" Abruptly he tossed his cigarette butt over the side of the car. "With another man's wife."

"Oh, Jerry!"

"I endorse that sentiment." His smile was cynical. "It's a lonely business, being in love with another man's wife."

So they sat, and they talked, and the half-hour Jerry had promised became unconsciously extended to two hours — two hours that went like the wind.

They got back to the party after everyone had gone home — everyone except Lew.

He sat in his overcoat at Olive's big piano, idly picking out a tune with one finger, a cigar in his mouth. Olive lounged in a low chair by the fireplace, the red skirts of her taffeta dress spread round her, her eyes, as they rested on Fay and Jerry in the doorway, frankly sympathetic.

Fay's heart was banging as she stood beside Jerry, gazing across at Lew, across this room that was stale with cigarette smoke, littered with smeared cocktail glasses and overflowing ashtrays. Her ride with Jerry had been entirely innocent, but the very set of Lew's shoulders, the aggressive way his cigar jutted from his mouth, made guilt and fear flower in her.

Then he rose lazily from the piano stool. "Ready to go home now?" he enquired of her, his eyes unfathomable as they rested on her frightened face, roamed her tumbled hair.

"Now look here, Lew," Jerry broke in, "don't go getting any ideas —"

"Ideas?" Lew was quietly folding his silk scarf into his overcoat. "What ideas should I get?"

"We merely went for a drive —"

"How very pleasant!" Lew turned to Olive. "Well, so long, Olive. We'll see you." He came over. His hand closed on Fay's arm and he drew her smoothly from the room.

He said not a word as they drove home, and Fay, frightened by his manner, couldn't have put two coherent words together. She knew how it must have looked and she shrank in her seat. The amused glances at Lew when, bored with playing poker, he came looking for her and she was no longer in her corner. Then someone would have told him, undoubtedly smiling, probably glad to see the high and mighty Lew Marsh put out of countenance for once: "Oh, she slipped out with Jerry Kaufmann — hours ago, my dear!"

With Jerry! Whom he hated!

As the lift rode to the top floor of Crystal Court, and they stepped out and walked to the door of the apartment, Fay shivered. It was a warm night, but she felt cold, inside and out.

Lew unlocked the door of the apartment and they stepped inside, Fay's hand moving automatically to the light switch. She walked drearily forward into the room and stood removing her silk wrap. Then, unable to bear any longer the silence that stood between them like a wall, she spoke. "Go ahead, Lew," she said, "tell me exactly what you think of me."

He didn't answer and she turned to look at him, her blue wrap half off her shoulders and exactly reflecting the color of her eyes. She looked strangely lovely then, gazing at him in half-fearful, half-apologetic defiance. "Oh, go ahead!" she cried. "I know you're annoyed with me. If we're going to quarrel because I went for an innocent little drive with Jerry, let's get it over with."

"Innocent drive?" he said, his mouth wry. "Was it really?"

Her blue eyes flashed. "If you're implying that it was anything else, then you're wrong. And insulting."

"You're gone for two solid hours with a guy like Kaufmann and you expect me to believe that it was all sweet niece and uncle?" he demanded.

"I do! We drove and drove. We didn't even talk much."

"Oh, I can well believe that you didn't talk much," Lew drawled.

As he said that, Fay began to tremble, but not with fear. Suddenly she was wildly angry. She swung away from him and made for her bedroom. How dare he imply that Jerry had made love to her! How dare he! Didn't Lew know her yet? Didn't he know that she could never, and would never, suffer any man's kisses but his? Another man's sympathy was one thing, but another man's lovemaking something she never even thought about, let alone wanted.

When she switched on the bedside light and looked at herself in the dressing-table mirror, she saw that she was as pale as the lillies of the valley at the neck of her dress. She unpinned the spray with fingers that shook, while Lew stood sternly in the doorway, his hands thrust into the pockets of his overcoat.

"If it had been any guy but Kaufmann, I'd believe you, Fay," he said. "But I refuse to believe that guy kept his hands off you for two solid hours. He isn't that self-controlled or that noble."

Fay swung round. "You refuse! You refuse!" she cried. "Well, I refuse to be accused of something I haven't done!"

But Lew only smiled, slowly and mockingly. "Why all the heat if you're telling the truth?" he drawled.

Temper flared wildly in Fay, burning away love, discretion, everything. "You're in no position to take away either my character or Jerry's! You're only the despicable swine who sent Inez Holden to her death!" she cried.

Lew was across the room in two strides then, gripping her shoulders so hard he bruised them. "Who told you that?" he demanded.

"Thalia Van Deen." Fay met his glittering eyes unflinchingly. "Weeks ago."

"I see. And you believed her, eh?"

"Well, it's the truth, isn't it? Even Pat Merryweather said it was true." The words broke recklessly, bitterly from Fay as she gazed up into Lew's eyes gone black and dangerous in a face where a sudden nerve of temper pulsed beside his mouth. "Thalia intimated that you treated that poor girl like dirt. She said you openly admitted at the inquest that you had — 'shown her the door.' "

"And your estimation of me now is that I'm an unrelieved swine, eh?" he spoke quietly and his eyes were losing their menacing glitter, cynicism creeping back into them. His gaze did not leave her face.

"Yes, Lew, that's my estimation of you exactly," she replied, wanting to hurt him; hoping she hurt him.

"What if I denied Thalia's story?" he enquired.

"You'd be wasting your time!" she flashed. "I'm not the starry-eyed little bumpkin you brought to Hollywood, Lew. You can't fool me any more. I know you now."

"You 'do, huh?" He watched her a moment longer, his face quite expressionless, then his hands dropped from her. He turned away and quietly collected his pyjamas, dressing gown and slippers. "I'll sleep in the other room tonight," he said. "Doubtless you'd prefer me to."

As the door closed on him, Fay stood very still, staring at the door, hardly daring to believe that he had gone — gone so quietly.

She undressed in a daze of misery; she was too miserable even for tears. She stood at the dressing-table brushing her hair, and her face, staring back at her from the mirror, was quite colorless. Lew would never forgive her — for saying it all — for knowing it all.

She laid aside the hairbrush and sank down on the bed, pressing her cold face to the cold silk of the cover-let. How strange his eyes had looked when she had cried aloud that girl's name! More startled, at first, than angry. Surely he must have realized that she'd get to hear the story sooner or later? In this town, this hotbed of gossip, it was the sort of tidbit that was bandied about all the time; if she hadn't heard it from Thalia, she'd have heard it from somebody else.

Yet now, remembering his startled eyes, the mask of awful anger that had come to his face, she knew a sudden regret that she had taunted him with her knowledge of Inez Holden. She lay prone on the bed, full of wild speculation as to how he would behave

89

toward her in the morning. Would he say they were through? Would he tell her to get out of his life? Her heart came into her throat.

Though he often hurt her with his impatience, his inability to understand how she could be reduced to tongue-tied nervousness by men he openly called jelly-bags, and women he scornfully labelled ambitious strumpets, there were other times when he put himself out to please her. Sometimes he took her out to dine at one of the quieter, less fashionable restaurants she liked, where they ate dinner in a dusky garden, under swinging lanterns, the scent of heliotrope and orange blossom all about them. Or took her out into the country in the car and chased her in the tall, sweet grass, thrusting handfuls of it down her back and laughing aloud at her breathless protestations.

She lay motionless, her face in her arms, emotion utterly spent in her. She no longer cared that Lew had chosen to believe that her moonlight drive with Jerry had been motivated by a desire for Jerry's love-making. All she knew was that she, swearing she loved Lew, had allowed her love to falter. While he, who had never promised love, had kept scrupulously to his side of the bargain.

Not once, in the few months of their marriage, had his interest strayed from her to another woman, yet she had seen exquisite creatures, golden-skinned from the beach, full of vivacious, sensuous appeal, throw openly inviting glances at him. He smiled at them, raising his black brows in quizzing, frank enjoyment of their beauty and their desire to flirt, but he went on holding her to his side with a firm brown hand.

What motivated his strange faithfulness — her likeness to Inez Holden? Her hand gripped the silk bedspread; her nails rasped upon the silk. . . .

She slept restlessly, lost and lonely in the big bed, missing Lew's hard, warm arms about her. When she awoke it was still very early, but she threw back the bedclothes and left the bed with thankfulness. Her night had been haunted by restless dreams and she was glad to get to the kitchen and busy herself with the making of breakfast.

As she carried breakfast into the sitting room, she examined Lew's face with apprehension. He was reading the paper and he didn't look up as she put his plate of bacon and eggs in front of him. Something that felt just like a walnut found its way into her throat, and when she took her seat at the opposite side of the table, she felt so unbearably unwanted that quick tears trembled on her lashes and she had to fight to stop them falling into her breakfast. Why didn't he speak? Anything was preferable to this awful silence. But he didn't speak, he just ate his usual sound breakfast, drank his usual three cups of coffee, and once again took up the paper at the sports section.

Fay, in a sudden excess of misery, pushed aside her untouched breakfast and rose to go to the kitchen, to get away from his impassive face. She was at the door when he said, "Don't forget we're going to the première of Bill's film tonight."

"Do you want me to go?" she asked, not turning to look at him.

She heard his chair scrape back and suddenly he was behind her, swinging her toward him. His dark face wore an irate impatience. "I don't intend to spoil Bill's bit of pleasure because we've had a row," he snapped. "The poor guy's been pretty sick these last few weeks and tonight's mighty important to him."

"All right, Lew," she said. "I'm not exactly keen to spoil Bill's evening myself."

"Excellent!" he retorted, and strode from the room, banging the door. A minute later she heard him leave the apartment.

CHAPTER NINE

THE foyer of the big cinema where the film of Bill Symans' novel, *Hunter's Moon*, was to be shown, was noisy and crowded, glittering with expensive jewelry, neon lighting and the dazzle of flashbulbs. The air was smoky and perfumed, and the excited burr of many voices rode above the sensuous rustle of silk and taffeta, shimmering under the fabulous gleam of mink.

Fay felt stunned by this wave of noise, brightness and perfume as she entered the foyer with Bill Symans and Lew. And she jumped nervously when a flashbulb seemed to explode right into her face. She heard Lew laugh and when she glanced up at him, he pulled a mocking face at her. "You have got the jumps tonight, my sweet," he murmured.

Embarrassed color swept into her cheeks. She rarely enjoyed these glamorous functions, but this one would be harder than most to get through.

She stood tensely between Lew and Bill, aware of painted eyes upon her, appraising her hair, set in a Grecian style at Olive Hadley's that afternoon; the wine-red velvet of her wrap, the jewels in her ears. She wanted to run out into the night. She didn't belong here. She was rejected on every side; even Lew rejected her!

As she lowered her head and bit at her lips to stop them from trembling, Bill's hand suddenly closed on her hand. He murmured, "Try pretending you're at the zoo. Pretend they're all a gorgeous set of beasts paraded for your mere amusement. I always do and it always works." A smile crept into his voice. "Look, d'you see that tall tigress in lemon and sable, the one who hasn't had any dinner — you can see she hasn't eaten, she's almost snarling? See that little parakeet in emerald? See that delicious squirrel with the turned-up nose and the button eyes?"

Fay had to laugh. "A few bars around them would make me feel a little easier," she confessed. She smiled up at Bill, grateful for his understanding. His thin face was very gentle, but it was also very tired and strained, and immediate concern caught at her heart. "Are you feeling all right, Bill?" she asked.

"Fit as a fiddle!" he retorted, but with a twinkle in his eye that frankly admitted he knew he wasn't fooling her.

Hunter's Moon was a psychological thriller, a beautifully produced, soundly acted film that would have held Fay's undivided attention had her mind not been on Bill half the time. His eyes wore a febrile luminosity tonight, and once, when he touched Fay's arm and murmured something about the film, his hand burned her dryly.

She watched him covertly, and when, halfway through the film, he quietly quitted his seat, she turned urgently to Lew. "I don't think Bill's very well," she whispered. "He's just gone out to the foyer."

Lew rose at once and the two of them hurried after Bill. He was sitting in one of the low gilt chairs ranged against the walls of the foyer, fighting to breathe and looking so ghastly that Lew said hurriedly to Fay. "I'll get a cab." He strode out through the swing doors of the cinema, past the gaping, noisy crowd that had gathered to see the coming and going of the many stars attending this première, and curious glances followed his tall, grim figure. A couple of girls giggled and called out after him, but he didn't hear them; wasn't even conscious of their presence.

He saw only Bill, half-fainting against the wine-red of Fay's wrap.

When they were in the cab, Bill said apologetically, "I feel a regular wet blanket, but you two chumps needn't have left the film, y'know."

"Never mind the film!" Lew exclaimed, watching Bill worriedly. There were gleaming fans of moisture in the deep scoops under Bill's eyes and his nostrils were waxen white and taut with pain. A flicker of affectionate amusement came into Bill's tired eyes as he met Lew's worried look. "You look all het up, old boy," he murmured. "Relax, there's a pal, I'm not going to croak, not yet."

But when they got to Bill's apartment, Lew took up the phone and called Bill's doctor. It wasn't only the look of Bill that prompted him, it was the professional watchfulness in Fay's eyes. He wasn't forgetting that she had been a nurse.

"You're making an awful lot of fuss, Lew," Bill protested. "I'm often like this. It passes." But his smile, as Fay carefully loosened his collar and removed his bow-tie, was a mere ghost of his usual cheerful one. "Where's the stuff you take for this, Bill?" Fay asked. "In the bathroom?"

"Cabinet. Top shelf." he answered.

She hurried to the bathroom, and it was as she reached up for the bottle of medicine that a sudden frightening feeling of dizziness seized her. She lay back against the cold tiles of the wall, fighting her weakness, breathing deeply, slowly, clinging to a solid world, a world that did not spin and lurch, with all her might. The white walls of the bathroom swam darkly and she rode dizzily on a wave of acute nausea, bathed in a cold sweat and icily afraid. It was minutes before she was again fully aware of the smooth coldness of the wall tiles under her pressing hands, the nervous hurrying of her heart.

She stood like a stone creature, spread-eagled against the wall, and the suspicion of a week or two slowly turned to certainty within her.

She was going to have a baby!

When she returned to the sitting room with Bill's medicine, she looked pale, but otherwise collected. She mixed the dose for him and watched him drink it, carefully stroking the fair hair back off his beaded forehead. "Feel a little easier?" she asked.

He nodded. "Um, that's very pleasant!" He lifted his own hand and held hers pressed to his forehead. "You've a nice cool hand, Fay. Cool hand, warm heart, don't they say?" His gray eyes dwelt on hers. "Lew's a darn lucky guy. Does he know it?"

She colored fiercely and was relieved when he turned his glance on Lew, who was sprawled out in an armchair, a whiskey and soda in his hand. His vital good looks, his dark vigor, were in strong contrast to Bill's febrile, brittle look, and Bill, as though realizing it, smiled sadly. "You're so darned healthy, you're almost disgusting, Lew," he said. "You make me feel like a weak old lady."

Lew didn't return Bill's smile. Instead he said harshly, "God plays funny tricks, putting pain and sickness in a guy like you and a houseful of health in a guy like me! I'd give up an arm to remedy that, I'd change places with you right now if I could."

"Now that's foolish kid talk, Lew, and you know it," Bill rejoined. "If I'm not bitter about all this, then you've no right to be so."

"Bitter!" Lew's chiselled face was a mask of bitterness. "I'm passionately bitter. I can't forgive the Almighty for what he's done to you." He stared down into the glass he held gripped in his hands. "The world's bound to be a rotten place, when everything good is taken out of it."

"That's a harsh philosophy, Lew." Bill was frowning.

"It's in all of us to be good or bad; weak or strong and God takes from every category. His is the final word on whatever happens to us and I refuse to question His word. There is doubtless a reason for all that He gives us or subjects us to. Glory in your strength, Lew; be grateful for all the sunshine that comes into your life and bear with the darkness."

But Lew was shaking his head and his dour glance left Bill and settled on Fay. "Sunshine merely settles on the skin, it doesn't penetrate, or so I've found," he murmured cynically. "Perhaps I deflect it, eh?"

When the doctor arrived, Lew drew Fay to one side and told her that she was to go home. "You're looking a trifle whacked," he said. "I'll hang on here until Bill feels a little better. Have you got enough money for the cab?"

She nodded.

"Go on, then," he said. "I shan't be late home."

As she ran down the steps of the apartment house and walked to the curb to hail a cab, a long cream Cadillac drew smoothly to a standstill in front of her and she found herself looking into the smiling gamin face of Jerry Kaufmann.

"Hullo, kid," he said. "Can I give you a lift?"

Fay stared at him, startled and uneasy. Last night he had been her best friend, but now that Lew had chosen to misinterpret that friendship, to see in it something guilty, Fay now felt guilty about it.

"Come on," Jerry opened the door of the car. "We've got things to talk about."

But still she hesitated. "How did you know I was here?" she asked.

"I was at the première. I saw you and Lew leave with Bill Symans. I followed the three of you. I've been hanging about here, hoping to get a glimpse of you." His voice dropped into a more intimate key. "I didn't dare to hope that I'd get to talk to you."

96

"Jerry — I daren't come with you!" she burst out.

His smile froze as he watched her. "Has Lew played heavy with you as well?"

"W — what do you mean?"

"He's had me pulled out of *Corn In The City*."

Her hand flew to her mouth in shocked distress. "Oh, no!"

"He's quite a boy, isn't he? Now do you feel like letting me give you a lift?"

She nodded dumbly. He reached over and drew her into the car beside him and as they pulled out from the curb he said, "I was going to keep away from you, Fay, then I saw you at the première tonight and bang went my good resolution." He glanced at her, his eyes almost melancholy. "I'm in love with you, Fay. I've been in love with you for weeks."

Her hands gripped on her bag. She gazed at him miserably. She didn't know what to say.

"Oh, don't go worrying about it!" He summoned up his old smile. "It's just one of those things. I'll tell you something, though. I'm a better guy than Lew Marsh. You might give that some consideration."

She bit her lip. "I'm — I'm sorry about the film, Jerry. I hope you're not out of work."

He laughed. "Oh, no! But I wasn't exactly pleased about being thrown out of that film. It was a darn good part."

They were silent then, until he turned the car into the circular drive of Crystal Court. But as the engine of the car ceased to purr, Jerry gently touched the wine-red velvet of Fay's wrap. "Look," he said, "are you really happy with Lew Marsh? Are you, Fay? I've got to know."

She looked away from him. She could feel his hand touching her wrap, smoothing the velvet. He was nice; he was gentle and kind, but his declaration of love had meant nothing at all to her.

97

"Of course I'm happy with Lew." She spoke carefully. "I understand him. I know he seems callous and hard, but — I understand him."

"You little, little fool!" Jerry whispered, and suddenly his arms were around her and he was drawing her against him, but when he tried to kiss her, she began to struggle. She pulled fiercely back from him, exerting all her strength. "Don't! Don't you dare!" she said, in a cold, hurrying whisper. "I don't want you! How dare you think I want you!"

His hands dropped from her. His gamin, expressive face showed his hurt. "I'm sorry!" he said. He watched her as she fumbled with the door of the car, as she stepped out on to the gravel of the drive. He watched her walk away, pass in through the swinging doors of Crystal Court. He sighed and sank back in his seat as the doors swung gently backwards and forwards, banishing her slim figure from his sight.

He sat very still for minutes on end. Once he drew out his cigarette case, and then dropped it back into his pocket. Suddenly he threw open the door of the car and he, too, went hurrying toward the swinging doors.

When the apartment bell rang, three times, peremptorily, Fay's nerves jumped.

She thought at once of Bill; perhaps Lew had sent over a message about Bill. But even as she was hurrying to the door, she was dismissing the thought. Lew would phone, he wouldn't waste time sending messages.

She opened the door and she stared at Jerry. Anger came washing back over her. "What do you want, Jerry? Haven't you finished pestering me yet?" she demanded.

He put his hand against the door, as though afraid she'd slam it in his face. "We haven't said everything yet, Fay," he spoke urgently, his almond eyes a warm, pleading brown. "We can't just turn away from each other, become strangers. I won't let that happen. Please let me come in! Let me talk to you!" His hand pressed more insistently on the door and he gently forced himself past her into the apartment. He closed the door and stood with his back to it.

"What's happened to us?" he asked. "We were pals. What's Lew said to you to make you turn against me?"

But she wouldn't answer, nervously twisting a chiffon handkerchief about in her hands, the diamonds of her wedding ring flashing under the gauzy material.

"I want to know, Fay. I've a right to know," he insisted repeatedly.

"Well, isn't it natural he should resent your attentions?" She threw back her head and met his eyes. "He is my husband."

Jerry's mobile mouth curled scornfully. "And just look at you — a picture of wedded bliss! A face as pale as a lily and eyes that have forgotten how to smile!" He looked her over, carefully, sadly. She wore a dress of soft, sheer, silver-gray wool, most beautifully embroidered in wine-red at the waist and at the neck. Small rubies gleamed in her ears. She looked delicately smart, delicately expensive.

"I can remember you the way you looked that day on the beach." Jerry smiled, gently. "You wore a lemon bathing suit and your hair was tied back with a piece of lemon ribbon. You looked like a little kid. I wanted to pick you up, then, and carry you off. Maybe I should have. I think you'd have come with me then."

And as he spoke of that day, she too remembered, and remembering, she smiled. "Perhaps I would have, Jerry," she admitted.

"And now it's too late?" he asked.

She nodded tiredly. "I married Lew. I married him knowing he only wanted a plaything, so I've myself to blame if he treats me as such. But a bargain's a bargain, so I shall stay with him for as long as he wants me to. It's as simple as that, you see, Jerry."

"But that isn't good enough!" Jerry stepped toward her, took and gripped her hands. His face was rather grim. "Fay, honey, you were made to be a man's pride, a man's pal! Someone for a man to laugh with and be friendly with. You weren't made to be shut up in a damned expensive apartment like some hothouse flower! I can give you joy! A ride on a roller coaster, an afternoon at the ball game. I know how to be a kid — and you know how to be one." His eyes implored her. "Come with me, honey! Come now, before it's too late. Before that guy kills every bit of laughing youth in you."

"But I love him!" She pulled her hands free of his. She stood before him, slim and fair and strangely poised. Her poise bewildered him. He preferred her shy gaucherie, her little-girl-lost air.

"You're enslaved by the guy!" he declared bitterly. "You'll wake up when it's too late — just like Inez did. He broke her, he'll do the same to you."

"I won't listen to talk like that," she cried angrily. "What right have you got to disparage Lew? Are you any better than he is?"

He frowned. A kind of wariness came into his eyes. "What do you mean by that?" he asked. "What's Lew said about me?"

"He implied that your reputation was on about the same level as his own, if you must know."

"And what do you think? Do you think that I'm in his class?" Jerry demanded.

She turned away wearily. She shook her head. "We're not getting anywhere, talking like this," she said. "We're only hurting one another. I'm sorry I can't love you, Jerry. I think it's a great pity I can't. But Lew's in my heart, for good or ill. I can't just push him out."

She felt Jerry's hand on her shoulder. "No, kid, as

you say, it isn't easy pushing someone out of your heart. I'm not going to find it easy, pushing you out. You crept in, with your little face and your big eyes." His voice softened. "I thought you liked me, Fay. You always danced in my arms as though you were real glad to be in them; as though they were some safe harbor you'd found in the middle of a storm."

Her heart seemed to turn right over as he said that. She turned to him in quick commiseration, and when he quietly put his arms round her, she let her head rest against his shoulder.

"I think I should have met you a long time ago, Jerry," she said.

"I wish to God you had!" For a moment his arms were fierce about her. "Fay — Fay, darling, don't let Lew Marsh hurt you. I shall be frightened all the time that he'll hurt you."

"Oh, Jerry, he isn't a monster." She smiled sadly, and then drew away from him. She lightly touched his cheek. "Now you'd better go. It's getting late."

"But what about us?" he asked. "Are only glimpses of you at premières and parties and in restaurants all I'm going to have of you?"

"I — I'm sorry, Jerry. I really am," she said. She didn't know what else to say.

"Okay!" He shrugged. He even produced something of his old merry grin. He walked to the door. He stood there, looking at her. "Are you sure you're not sending away the wrong guy?" he asked.

She shook her head.

"I think maybe you are, kid," he said. Then he quietly let himself out of the apartment.

CHAPTER TEN

Lew was late coming in, but Fay was still up, waiting for him. As he strode in, throwing off his overcoat, he stared, seeing her curled up among the scarlet cushions on the big couch. "Why aren't you in bed?" he asked.

"I wasn't sleepy," she said. "How's Bill? What did the doctor say?"

"He's got to go into hospital." Lew sighed as he came over to her and stood looking down at her. "He won't come out, Fay. He's going to die in that hospital. He's thirty-three. He hasn't begun to live — to do half the things he was meant to do. He's such a good guy. Why should it happen to him?"

"I don't know, Lew. Time and time again, when I was nursing, I've seen it happen, and the sadness of it never lessened for me. I know just how you feel. It's not being able to do anything to stop it. It's such a depressing, impotent feeling, isn't it?"

He nodded.

She rose and touched his arm. "Would you like some coffee?" she asked.

He smiled at her quietly. "Yes, please!"

She went out to the kitchen and made coffee and ham sandwiches, and when she carried in the tray, Lew was standing at the window, staring out into the night. With his back to her, he looked very tall, very broad. Fay watched him, wondering again at the complexity of his nature. Only tonight she had learned that out of pure spite he had had Jerry Kaufmann taken out of *Corn In The City*. Yet he stood there, staring into the darkness, filled with compassion for Bill, torn with impotent bitterness because there was nothing he could do to hold back the swift wings of death, so soon to close over the gentle integrity of Bill.

"Come and drink your coffee while it's hot, Lew," she said.

He turned and came to her, throwing himself down beside her on the couch. She handed him his coffee and he stirred sugar into its steaming blackness; he never took cream in his coffee. "By the way," he said, "I'm going to England in a few weeks' time."

"England?" She stared at him. England! Green fields with an early morning mist on them. The lazy sound of church bells of a Sunday afternoon. The warm tinkle of teacups through an open window. But he had said, "I'm going to England. . . ." He hadn't said "We're going. . . ."

"Directly *Corn In The City* is in the can I'm going over." He sipped his coffee. "K.C. wants to do Shakespeare's *The Rape of Lucrece*, and I can't help admitting I'm enthusiastic. It's a darned tricky story, of course, but if we bring if off — wow!" Lew's dark eyes gleamed. "I'm going to Stratford-on-Avon to try and persuade a certain English actor who rusticates there to come out of retirement and play Tarquin."

"What about censorship, Lew?" Fay asked. "As you say, it's a tricky story."

"That is the rub," Lew admitted, smiling a little and biting into a sandwich, "but Karl can afford the loss, if it turns out a loss, and I'll have had the artistic satisfaction of directing an expensive box office flop. It's funny, but Shakespeare, with all its passion, never does too well at the box office. And d'you know why? Because most people are fools. They shrink like violets from good, honest passion, which, if only they'd be honest and admit it, is all they feel themselves in the name of love. They will wrap sex up in pretty, piffling declarations of love. The big, tough hero must carry his mate off into the bush, but by heaven, if he doesn't say, afterwards, 'I love you, darling' — cut! The censor is swooning. Or the public are."

"Well, Lew, it's human nature to like pretty wrappings," Fay protested. "A girl in silk, a birthday present in a colored box, a pair of lamb chops in frilly leggings. Life would be as blunt as the back of a knife without a few pretentions, and well you know it."

He stared at her, then he put back his head and laughed.

"Right on the chin — whacko! You've quite a punch, for all that you're a feather-weight."

And as he sat laughing, she said, "Why have you had Jerry Kaufmann taken out of *Corn In The City*?"

His laughter faded abruptly. "So you know about that?"

"I saw Jerry — tonight."

"Really? What was his version of the story — that I had him thrown out of the film because he was after you?"

Color stung her cheeks. "I imagine you did it out of spite!" she retorted, coldly.

"What a delightful opinion you have of me, Fay." He was smiling quizzically as he helped himself to more coffee. "I wonder you can bear to sit in the same room with me."

She turned her head away, biting her lip at the words.

"The truth is," he went on, "Kaufmann and I couldn't work together; it was spoiling the film. I don't let spite sway me, Fay, and you can believe me or disbelieve me, but I promise you I shan't start crying into my coffee if you do the latter."

As he sipped his coffee, he studied her averted head, the delicate curve of her profile. He saw her slight

104

breast lift on a sigh. "Say it, Fay." He spoke mockingly. "Say you've stopped loving me."

Slowly her head turned and her blue eyes bleakly examined his face. "If it pleases you to take my wings off, do it, Lew," she murmured.

"Is it guilt or martyrdom induces you to make the offer?" he queried.

She stared at him. "I wonder why I love you," she whispered. "You're as hard as iron, aren't you?"

"If you say so," he replied. He set aside his coffee cup and as he leaned back in the couch, his hand swooped and his fingers closed like springs on her wrist. Deliberately he jerked her to him, so that she fell down upon his chest. Before she could elude him, his other hand was upon her waist and he was holding her immovable against him. "I'm sorry I can't be the knight in shining armor you seem to want, but I'm as good to you as I know how to be." His lips quirked. "I'm nicer to you than I am to a lot of people."

She stared up into his eyes, above which the black brows curved so wickedly; she felt the strong beat of his heart against her and she was acutely conscious in that moment that she carried his child. She wondered what he'd say, how he would react, if she imparted that fact to him here and now. Would he show her tenderness, or would he be discomfited that their transitory marriage was going to produce a child?

"What are you thinking?" he suddenly asked.

"Nothing." She attempted to pull away from him. "I'm tired, Lew. Let me go to bed."

"A while ago you were claiming you weren't sleepy," he mocked. "What's the matter, my darling, are you afraid I'm going to force my passionate attentions upon you? Is my touch less thrilling now that you've sampled Kaufmann's?"

"You're despicable!" She was struggling wildly in his arms. "Let me go! For God's sake let me go!"

"I'm damned if I will!" Suddenly his face was harsh. "I've got something to say first; while you stay under my roof, you'll keep away from Kaufmann, understand? You're my wife and you'll do what I say. You once accused me of buying you. All right, Fay, I bought you! I bought your affection, and while it pleases me to enjoy that affection, I'll enjoy it, but I'll enjoy it exclusively — and when it suits me to." Abruptly he turned her in his arms and forced her head back against the cushions of the couch. His lips came to her throat, fierce in the delicate hollow of her throat, and now she lay passive, dumb with misery.

"Is this submission or disinterest?" he murmured, mockery back in his voice.

"How can you believe I want Jerry Kaufmann? How can you believe it?" She almost moaned the words in her torment.

"I'm as entitled to believe what I believe as you are," he replied cryptically.

The following day Fay went to see a doctor and had the fact that she was pregnant definitely confirmed.

The doctor was a youthful, hulking man, who watched her across his desk with friendly, questioning eyes. "What's worrying you, Mrs. Marsh?" he asked, in a soft, slow voice, a voice that came strangely from his bull frame, his big, clefted jaw. "Kids can be great fun, you know. I've got three."

"Three!" Fay stared at him in amazement. He looked so young. He barely looked married.

He smiled. "Start young and they grow up with you," he said. "It's the only way. They don't go getting these modern notions that because they have to call you 'pa' you're decrepit." He grew serious. "When I first confirmed your pregnancy your eyes lit up. Now, why are you looking sad?" He leaned his elbows on the desk. "Look, are you thinking that maybe your husband won't want this baby? I know lots of men get these notions. They think that once the kids start coming, they're going to get neglected; no more affection — the baby will get it all. Is that what you're worried about, Mrs. Marsh?"

She picked at the leather of her handbag with her fingernail. If only it were as simple as that, she thought.

"I guess that is my — my worry," she murmured almost incoherently.

"Well," he said, a smile breaking over his face, "you go home and make such a fuss of the darned boob, he'll think it's his birthday. He'll want kids all the time."

Then he grew a little more technical. He said carefully, "I'm bound to tell you this, Mrs. Marsh, but I don't want you to go getting any silly notions that you're ill or anything. The fact is, some women are made to bear a dozen children, it comes as easy to them as whipping up dinner. But others — well, they aren't quite so fortunate—"

"You mean that I'm in the latter category?" Fay interjected quietly.

"I'm afraid so," he admitted. "You're definitely going to have to watch yourself. Take exercise, but don't overdo it. Some dancing won't hurt, but midnight balls are out, and so is any extensive travelling. A lot of women can do all these things and thrive on them, but you won't be able to."

Fay gazed at him in consternation. "Don't tell me I've got to behave like an invalid!" she exclaimed.

He smiled at once, shaking his head. "Heavens, no! Just take life a little slower, a little easier, especially for these first few months. And I want you to come and see me regularly."

Fay walked from the doctor's office in something of a daze. Perhaps it was just as well Lew hadn't asked her to go to England with him. No extensive travelling! The fates were really combining to separate her from Lew — even if he asked her now, she would have to refuse.

Then, three weeks later, Bill Symans died.

Although it was something both Fay and Lew had expected, it still came as a shock. They attended the funeral along with dozens of other people. Bill had been more than liked, he had been loved, and Fay was disturbed to see people who looked as though they hadn't a tear in them break down and cry when the beautiful coffin was lowered into the dark soil.

Throughout the funeral Lew remained calm, but when he and Fay got back to the apartment, his impassivity broke. He didn't say a word, he just left her, shut himself in the spare bedroom with a bottle of whiskey and drank himself into oblivion.

Fay was neither surprised nor disgusted. She had known all along that he wouldn't take Bill's death with equanimity.

She left him alone until about nine o'clock; then she made coffee and took it into him. He lay sprawled across the bed, his hair in disorder, his tie pulled loose from the collar of his shirt, his jacket in a heap.

Fay put the coffee tray down on the bedside table and sat down on the bed, lifting his black head and cradling him against her. She could smell the whiskey on his breath, but she wasn't revolted, and when, with an inarticulate murmur, he pressed his face to her and clung to her, she laid her cheek against his hair and gently rocked him.

"I know, my darling. I know how you feel," she whispered. "It hurts, losing someone you love. It's desolation — it's bitter eating. I know, Lew."

They stayed like that for many minutes, then, with a sigh, he drew away from her. He lay looking up at her, his eyes smeared and bloodshot from the whiskey.

"I'll be glad to get away from this place," he said, his

voice muted and thick. "I can't wait for us to go."

She stared down at him. "You — want me to come?" she asked.

"Of course you're coming!" Impatience moved in his eyes. "What did you think, that I was going to leave you all alone in this place? I'm not that low."

Fay moved thoughtfully off the bed and stood pouring coffee. Dr. Forrester had said she was to do no extensive travelling — yet Lew's need of her cried out so hard that all other voices were drowned, lost. For the first time in their relationship he really needed her. It was in the way he sat pushing the rumpled hair back from his face, the hardness gone from his mouth and a boyish, hurt droop in its place. In the way, as she handed him his coffee, his eyes lifted and met hers, a silent pleading in them.

If she told him about the baby, he would go to England alone.

But she couldn't tell him, for his eyes were lonely — lonelier than she could ever have believed they could look. He wanted her to go with him and it wasn't in her to refuse him.

A few days before they left for England, Fay went to see Dr. Forrester. She explained about the trip. She emphasized Lew's uneasy acceptance of his friend, Bill Symans' death. "I can't see him go alone," she said.

"You'll be risking your child, Mrs. Marsh," he warned.

"Oh, but we'll be flying." Her eyes begged him to understand. "It isn't such a very long trip. Surely — surely —"

"If you take my advice, you'll stay home." He spoke gravely.

But she shook her head. "Lew comes first," she said.

CHAPTER ELEVEN

FAY stood and watched the fountain that played in the Avon. To her left the very modern Shakespeare Memorial Theatre was reflected in all its clean simplicity of line in the clear water of the lake, but Fay, at this moment, was only aware of the cold English wind blowing along the lakeside and of the leaves scurrying in the grass at her feet.

She shivered and drew the fur collar of her dark red coat closer about her face. How much longer was Lew going to be? When he had suggested that she might enjoy taking a walk around the town instead of sitting in on a boring technical conference, just around the corner, she had agreed. But the conference, made up of various film men interested in this Shakespearean venture of Karl Christbel's, including the actor Lew had come in particular to see had now lasted two hours, and Fay was beginning to feel very cold and rather hungry.

She opened her bag and took out her cigarette case. She lit herself a cigarette, nervously aware of the tremor that kept running through her, affecting in particular her legs. They felt, every now and again, as though they were going to buckle up under her. She drew deeply on her cigarette, coughing a little as the smoke sawed her throat.

It was March.

March in England, with clouds like white puffs of meringue blowing along in a rather fitful sky; with a nip in the air that Fay was very conscious of after her seven months in the much warmer climate of Hollywood.

The smoke of her cigarette drifted away over the Avon and strands of her fair hair were whipped across her forehead by the wind. She didn't hear quiet footsteps approach behind her and when a smiling, well-known voice murmured in her ear, "I know a shop, kid, where the pastries are works of art and the tea sheer nectar, how about coming with me and trying them?" She was so startled that all she could do for at least a minute was stand and stare — straight into the warm, almond-shaped eyes of Jerry Kaufmann.

Then warmth was flooding her, bringing her back to life, brightening her eyes back to their usual vivid blue. "Jerry! You!"

He swept her a gallant little bow. "None other, my queen."

"Oh, Jerry, you absurd fool!" She laughed, she touched his arm, as though to make sure he was real. "What are you doing here — of all places?"

He grinned merrily. "Taking in the wonders of Stratford-on-Avon. Supping a little of its famous air. Why not?" His eyes, moving over her face, were openly fond. "Gee, seeing you again does me good!" he exclaimed.

"Oh, Jerry!" she laughed, breathlessly. "I can't get over this! I was feeling so — so down — and you turn up!"

"Like a bad penny?" he queried quizzically.

"No! Oh, no!" She caught at his arm. "I couldn't be more pleased. But what are you doing in England?"

"Come and eat pastries with me and I'll tell you," he said.

"That would be nice — but I don't know whether I can." She smiled. "I'm waiting for Lew."

"Where is the guy?"

"Winding up a business deal. When Lew gets talking about moving pictures and camera angles, I fade right into the background." She looked rueful. "I believe he's forgotten he brought me with him."

"And you're darned bored and darned hungry," Jerry finished for her.

She nodded.

Very deliberately then, he took hold of her arm. "You're coming with me," he said, in a voice that showed he didn't intend to brook any argument. "I'm going to introduce you to some solid pudding and beef."

"But you said pastries," she objected. "They sounded lovely."

"It's red beef and gravy you need, kid." He eyed her, concernedly. "I believe you're shivering. What's that guy thinking of, leaving you hanging about here in the cold?" And without further ado, he turned her and marched her across the sparse, shaven grass towards the steps that led up to the pavement.

They ate a very solid lunch and then, over coffee, he told her why he had come to England.

"I've landed a very nice contract with Suvia Pictures," he explained. "They're a European company. I like the pictures they make and they seem to like me, so it's a real love match. I was kind of getting in a rut in Hollywood, playing the same sort of parts all the time. I'll spread my wings with Suvia." He grinned at her over his coffee cup. Very deliberately he said, "D'you know, you're even prettier than I remember you."

She ignored the compliment. "What are you doing in Stratford?" she asked.

"I'm here to steal Lew Marsh's wife," he replied.

"You're what?"

"You heard, honey."

"Are you mad? I thought you'd forgotten all that nonsense, Jerry."

"It isn't nonsense to me, I love you, Fay — I'm out to get you."

"But what I said to you back in Hollywood still goes, Jerry." She looked earnest. "Why should you think I've changed?"

He shrugged. "You're going to one day. The spell that guy's woven about you has got to break one day. I want to be around when it does. That's why, every now and again, I'll pop up at your elbow, like a genie." He grinned engagingly.

As they strolled back towards the Memorial Theatre, they saw Lew. He was pacing up and down on the green that fronted the lake, smoking a cigar and looking impatient. He stared, his black brows pulling down when he saw who accompanied Fay, holding her arm as they crossed the road.

He strode towards them. "Where have you been?" he demanded of Fay.

She smiled up at him, fighting her apprehension. He looked in a temper, his mouth thin, his nostrils pulled in imperiously. "I was cold and hungry, and Jerry appeared out of the blue and offered me lunch," she explained, the words tumbling out of her mouth, so eager was she to conciliate him.

"You could have come over to the hotel — if you were that cold and hungry. Anyone would think I'd deliberately neglected you," he said curtly. And as color moved in her cheeks, he turned his irate glance on Jerry. "What are you doing in Stratford? Getting culture?" he asked sarcastically.

Jerry faced him imperturbably. "I'm doing a tour," he said, airily. "I went to see Warwick Castle yesterday. Now that's quite a place! You two ought to go."

"I doubt whether we'll have the time," Lew replied, coldly. "We're going back to London tonight."

"Oh, are we?" Fay broke in. "I thought we were staying on here a few more days?"

113

"Well, we aren't!" He reached over and drew her to his side. "You'd better tell your little playmate goodbye. I've got to get back to the hotel and make a few phone calls."

Fay bit her lip. She looked at Jerry and saw that his eyes were still unconcernedly smiling. "Goodbye, Jerry!" she murmured obediently. "I hope you like working with Suvia Pictures."

"I shall, kid," he assured her. With an almost imperceptible wink at her and a final puckish glance at Lew, he strolled away, his hands thrust into the pockets of his raincoat. Fay watched him go, a queer, sharp feeling of pain at her heart. The day seemed suddenly colder now that the warm friendliness always emanating from Jerry had been withdrawn. She turned resentfully to Lew. "Why do you always have to be so rude to Jerry?" she demanded.

"Why do you always have to care that I am rude?" he countered.

"Because he's a friend of mine. Oh, don't sneer, Lew! Just because you dislike Jerry, do I have to?"

He took her arm and marched her across the road. "You're just flattered because he's following you around."

"He's doing nothing of the sort!" She looked indignant — perhaps that much more indignant because there was a certain amount of truth in what Lew said. "He's here to make pictures."

"He's following you around," Lew reiterated. "You've really made an impression on him, haven't you?" He glanced down at her, his eyes mocking. "Well, he's going to have to wait just a little longer. I'm afraid I'm not quite ready yet to hand you over to him."

She flushed and pulled her arm free of his hand. "Don't be beastly to me because your darned business talk wasn't to your liking," she said, voicing a

114

suspicion she had had from the moment she had seen him pacing along the lakeside. Although he hadn't been too pleased to see her with Jerry, that impatient, tigerish pacing had been part of something else. She had seen it before — and always in connection with his work. If things didn't go too well at the studios, he'd invariably come home and pace the sitting room carpet till his temper cooled.

Now he proved her surmise a correct one. With abrupt apology, he took her arm again and pulled her to his side as they walked towards their hotel. "I'm sorry, Fay," he said. "I guess I am sore. That guy Brewster won't play ball." His voice grew caustic. "He says acting bores him, it always has, he's now found his true vocation — farming! Would you believe it? The guy prefers to grow cabbages! And Karl isn't offering him peanuts to play lead in *Lucrece*."

Lew was still on about Ralph Brewster as they sped toward London that evening, in the car he had hired for their trip to Stratford. He wasn't used to right-hand driving and every so often the car gave a sickening jerk, stirring anew in Fay the slight feeling of nausea she had had, on and off, all day.

The feeling worried her. She had grown used to experiencing some discomfort first thing in the morning, but that usually wore off after she had been up and about for an hour, but today it had been present almost continually, along with that queer, weak aching in her legs.

She leaned back in her seat, forcing herself to relax, to ignore Lew's rather precarious driving. "You talk, Lew, as though Ralph Brewster's the only actor who could possibly play Tarquin," she said.

"He's one of them," Lew grunted. "He's got personality, presence and physique. When you can combine those three things, along with experience and talent, you're way inside the box office, believe me."

"Well," Fay said, smiling, "if that's what you need, play Tarquin yourself. You'd make a perfectly awesome Tarquin. You'd stop a million hearts without any trouble at all."

But Lew wasn't in the mood for frivolous remarks. It hadn't pleased him in the least that he had been unable to talk Brewster into accepting the lead in this Shakespearean film. He honestly believed that with Brewster playing lead, the film stood a tolerable chance of being successful. He was known in America — half the battle — and he possessed a verve and a dash that was lacking in a lot of English actors of Brewster's eminence. It had been his idea; he had suggested it to Karl Christbel, that they star Brewster in *Lucrece*.

Suddenly he said to Fay, "D'you know, I'm not going to give up! I've a good mind to go back to Stratford and have another go at that guy."

"Tonight?" She gazed at him in consternation. She felt tired and sick and worried. And that warning of Dr. Forrester's — that if she came on this trip to England she might very well lose her baby — had been in her mind all day. She reached over and gripped Lew's arm. "Can't we stop overnight somewhere and go back in the morning?" she begged.

He glanced at her, frowning. "D'you feel tired, then?" he asked.

She nodded.

"Look," he said, "I think we're near Thame. How would it be if I got you fixed up at a pub for the night? I can easily go back alone if you don't fancy the journey."

"But surely that isn't necessary, Lew?" she protested. "Surely you can wait until the morning?"

But his mouth had set obstinately. "I like to do things while my mind's made up on them," he said. "I'm darned if I'll take 'no' from that guy! I'm going

116

back tonight. You can stop in Thame or you can come with me. Suit yourself."

And Fay, unutterably weary of the jolting of the car, aware that she'd be sick in earnest if she had to bear much more of it, chose to let him find her a decent pub in Thame where she might stay overnight.

As he saw her settled in, as he prepared to leave her, he said, "Expect me about lunch time tomorrow." He grinned. "I shan't forget I've left you here."

"All right." She stood gazing up at him, looking and feeling rather forlorn. "Aren't you going to kiss me?" she asked.

"D'you want me to?" His eyes questioned her and she saw now that though the problem of Ralph Brewster had predominated in his thoughts all afternoon, he hadn't quite forgotten Jerry Kaufmann's sudden appearance in Stratford. He was still a little suspicious of that appearance of Jerry's she realized.

"Of course, I want you to," she murmured.

"You don't usually ask me," he countered.

"I don't usually have to," she retorted.

He laughed then and drew her toward him, drew her close into his arms. As he bent his head to hers, she clasped her arms about his neck and clung to him.

The power and strength of that kiss, exchanged there in that quaint, dim bedroom, smelling of mothballs, left Fay a little dazed. She lay with her head against his shoulder, his arms tight about her.

"You kissed me as though I were marching away to the wars," he murmured, trying to speak lightly, but in truth, almost as shaken as she was.

"I — know. I wonder why?" She drew back and looked up at him, a strange apprehension moving in her eyes. She wanted to say, "Don't go, Lew! Please don't leave me!" but she held back the words, though it cost her something to hold them back.

"Are you all right?" he suddenly asked her, watching her and wondering at her pallor, her almost exhausted look. He couldn't make out why she should look so wan. They had done no mad gallivanting. These three weeks in England had been the quietest they had known since their marriage. "Don't you feel well, Fay?" He touched her cheek, feeling its coldness.

"I'm tired, that's all," she reassured him. "You go and see Brewster. Turn on all your charm."

"You're — sure?" he said.

She nodded.

"Get to bed early, honey," he urged, then he lightly pinched her chin and left her.

CHAPTER TWELVE

FAY washed and tidied herself and went down to the bar parlor to eat her solitary dinner.

The landlord of the pub was vastly concerned that she should be eating alone. "It's being so early on in the season," he said. "We rarely get many overnight visitors this time of the year."

"Oh, don't worry about me," she said, smiling at him. "I'm perfectly happy."

But he wouldn't be consoled. "Now it wouldn't be so bad for you if the young American gent was coming down to dinner, but he didn't order any dinner."

Fay blinked as she digested this. "The young American gent wouldn't be called Mr. Kaufmann, would he?" she asked. And even before the landlord nodded his florid head in confirmation, she knew that the other visitor was Jerry. To have picked the same pub as Jerry!

"I take it you know the young gent, miss?" the landlord said.

"Oh yes, Mr. Kaufmann and I are old friends. We've both been in Stratford, having a look round. It's a fine place, isn't it?"

" 'Tain't the place it used to be," the landlord of the Swan and Maid returned dourly. "All that there catering for tourists has spoilt the place."

After Fay had eaten her dinner, she sat reading magazines on the leather-cushioned settee that stood near the big fireplace, where a fire roared cheerfully. The warmth was very pleasant against her legs and some of her earlier weariness faded as she relaxed in the quiet of the pub.

She was absorbed in an article on old English castles, when the door breezed open and cheery masculine whistling died on a note of extreme surprise.

Fay glanced up, her dimples well to the fore as she examined Jerry's incredulous face. "Yes, it's me," she said.

"Where's Lew?" he asked, as he came across the room to her, glancing round as though expecting to see Lew in hiding behind one of the big carved chairs or behind the floral curtains at the windows.

She laughed. "Lew's deposited me here like a parcel and gone back to Stratford," she explained.

Jerry stared. "On the level? What's so interesting in Stratford?"

"Ralph Brewster. Lew wants him under contract, but he's proving obstinate. And you know Lew, he won't rest until he gets his own way."

"Too true!" Jerry pulled a face. "Say, let's you and me have a drink. Tomato juice, huh?"

"That would be nice," she agreed.

He returned with tomato juice for her and brimming rustic ale for himself. He sat down beside her on the settee and she felt his eyes moving over her as she held her tall glass of juice and sipped it. His openly admiring appraisal embarrassed her and she said quickly, "You haven't told me why you're here."

"My car broke down." He grinned at her. "I said a few cuss words at the time, but I'm blessing that axle now. Lew won't bless it, though, I bet."

"If you're going to start saying mean things about Lew, I'm not going to sit here and talk to you," Fay informed him, with perfect seriousness.

"Okay, okay! We'll talk about you instead. Why aren't you the skinny little thing you used to be?"

The question took her breath, and then she blushed vividly. Lew had not noticed the slight alteration in her contours, but Jerry, not having seen her for some weeks, had noticed, and it was typical of him to frankly comment on the fact. He had always had an enthusiastic, rather boyish tendency to say the first thing that came into his head.

He watched the quick blooming of her blush and its slow fading and he frowned. Gradual comprehension stirred in the depths of his eyes, growing and becoming certainty as her lips moved tremulously on the rim of her glass of tomato juice.

"I'll guess in a minute," he said.

"Go ahead and guess," she retorted, smiling.

"Lew, it seems, has all the luck!" Jerry's grin held irony. "Is he pleased at the prospect of fatherhood?"

"He doesn't know yet."

Jerry looked astonished. "Saving the news for his birthday?" he queried.

Fay's glance faltered from his, but Jerry's hand was immediately at her chin, tilting her face up. "What's up, kid? Aren't things going too well?"

But instead of answering his question, she asked one. "Did you know Inez Holden, Jerry?"

He nodded and released her chin. "Yeah, I knew Inez. Why do you ask?"

She nervously twisted and turned the tall glass that held her drink. "I — I sometimes wonder if Lew still thinks about her."

"You think he might have her on his conscience?" Jerry's gamin face was suddenly hard. "He ought to."

"Tell me all about it, Jerry." Fay's hand reached for his arm. "I must know exactly what Lew did to that girl to make her do — such a terrible thing."

"You mean commit suicide?"

Fay nodded, her eyes big on his face.

And then, abruptly, he set aside his beer tankard

121

and stood up. He began to pace the rather worn strip of carpet that lay in front of the fireplace. "I haven't much time for Lew Marsh," he said, "but I do care for you, Fay. I care to this extent," he came and stood over her, "I care enough to say the thing I wouldn't say three years ago, when a verdict of suicide was brought in on Inez Holden." He held her gaze, his almond-shaped eyes flashing. "Inez didn't commit suicide."

Fay stared up at him. "How do you know?"

"I was with her at the time."

He straightened up and took his cigarette case from his pocket. He extended it to Fay, but she shook her head, watching him light a cigarette, noticing that his hand was shaking slightly.

"Inez and I were friends before she ever met Lew." He spoke quietly, dispassionately. "I wasn't in love with her, but I liked her. Then she met Lew at a party and shortly afterward they got engaged. From all accounts he wanted to get married right away, but she was eager to get into movies and make a name for herself first."

Jerry shrugged and drew hard on his cigarette. "The trouble was, she couldn't act, but she was beautiful. When you looked at her you thought of lily pools and flower gardens and white moonlight. I guess Lew was pretty infatuated with her at that time, for he got Karl Christbel to put her under contract. He even got her a part in a film he was directing at that time.

"It was called *Come Tenderly, My Sweet*, but the moment Inez stepped into the film, things seemed to go haywire. She was like a jinx on it. Janie Streeter, who was playing female lead, went down with a virus and had to be replaced. A whole can of exposed film went up in flames, along with one of the projection rooms and a pile of expensive scenery, and it was only

Lew's influence with old Christbel that stopped him tossing Inez out on her ear. K. C.'s a superstitious guy, and directly he got it into his head that it was Inez who was jinxing the film, he took to hating her. And it was probably knowing she was in bad with K. C. that made Inez's acting go from bad to rotten.

"Then Casey Anderson, who was playing male lead, did a sit-down strike. He told Lew that if Inez didn't get her walking orders, he'd walk out. It wasn't that Casey objected to Inez's bad acting, it was because she didn't like him and his tendency to make passes at her in dark corners, and she had told him so, in front of the entire cast of the film. But Casey, as Lew well knew, had to be considered. He was sure fire box office at that time and Lew was never a guy to be swayed by sentiment."

Jerry smiled slightly as he studied Fay's small, intent face. He had heard it remarked that she resembled Inez; he supposed she did to a certain extent. But whereas Inez's mouth had sometimes expressed petulance and impatience, Fay's was always a gentle, glowing curve, eminently kissable. He sighed as he resumed his story.

"So Lew told Inez that she'd never be more than a pretty piece of decoration. He told her that the only part she could ever play with anything approaching efficiency was the profile on a penny. He told her that Casey was in and she was out. God knows why he had to tell her in such brutal terms, but Lew's kind haven't a lot of patience with mediocrity and I guess he was pretty well fed up with the way Inez had spoiled scene after scene of *Come Tenderly, My Sweet* with her bad acting. He informed her that he wouldn't have put up with five minutes of it if she hadn't been wearing his ring. So Inez tossed the ring in his face, told him to do what he liked with it. He put his heel on it and ground it to smithereens."

Jerry lit himself another cigarette, his thumb impatient on the wheel of his lighter.

"I heard all about the fight from Inez, later that same day, when we met in a downtown bar. She was feeling reckless and drinking hard. I didn't try to stop her. She needed to drink. I've sometimes needed it myself. When life gets hold of you by the throat, the only way out sometimes is to drink until fireworks start or black oblivion comes. With Inez it was fireworks. When we left that bar she was like a sparkling, crazy torch, not caring about anything or anyone. We went dancing. We rode through the park in a landau. Maybe I came close to thinking I loved her that night — I don't know." Jerry shrugged and tossed ash off his cigarette. "Anyway, when she suggested I go back to her apartment with her, I went."

. He smiled cynically at Fay. "She was beautiful. She was also Lew Marsh's girl. I didn't like him, y'see. I never did. Maybe because everything seemed to come to him so easily. Maybe because he never had to claw his way to the top, like I did. I guess I hated, too, his ability to go through life treading on people's toes and not having them care — or, if they cared, not caring himself.

"Well, it went on like that for a week or more, Inez and I hitting the high spots, and then, all at once, she seemed to come to her senses. One night, we'd been to a movie, and as we left the cinema, Inez suddenly said, quite seriously, that she was going to see Lew. She was going to ask him to take her back. Life was empty without him, she said. So I drove her to his place and waited. Somehow I knew that she was running to a dry well; that Lew Marsh's high and mighty pride wouldn't tolerate any backsliding in a girl he intended to marry. And I was right."

Jerry stared straight into Fay's wide blue eyes. Cinders rolled from the fire into the grate and the distant

124

hum of male voices talking in the saloon bar came to them.

"Inez was crying as she came running out of Crystal Court. I was on the opposite side of the road, sitting in my car. I saw exactly what happened. She stepped off the curb to come to me — and went straight under the wheels of a truck. At the inquest, Lew openly admitted that he had thrown Inez out of his apartment. The driver of the truck said that she walked under his wheels, and I was in no mood to dispute the statement. I agreed with it."

"And they called it suicide," Fay said quietly.

Jerry nodded.

"Why did you do that to him, Jerry? Why?"

"Because she took her love to him, and her broken pride, and he threw them back in her lovely face."

Fay shivered, her clenched hands cold as ice. "Lew has pride," she murmured.

"He's hard, all the way through." Jerry bent and lightly touched her cold hands. "What is it that makes you love him, Fay? What makes you love a man who hasn't an ounce of compassion or understanding in him?"

"I don't know — I don't know."

"I can be both, Fay." He spoke quietly, almost wistfully. "I'll take you now, if you'll come."

"I'm having his baby, Jerry."

"I said I'll take you, if you'll come."

But she shook her head. "Leave me alone, Jerry," she pleaded. "Please leave me alone."

"All right." He straightened up, tossing his cigarette butt into the dying fire. "All right, kid. I'll go for now, but we'll meet again — we're meant to meet again."

"Are we, Jerry?" She gazed straight up into his gamin face, as though she would absorb every detail — almond eyes, humorous mouth, black curls drifting down upon his forehead. "Thank you for telling me the real truth about Inez Holden, Jerry," she said.

"I'd give you the world — you've only to ask." Then he lightly touched his curls in a farewell salute. "I'm leaving first thing in the morning, so I'll say goodbye now, Fay."

"Goodbye, Jerry."

The door closed and Fay's rather melancholy glance moved back to the fire, and for long moments, enclosed by the silence of the room, she stared into the fire. Lew believed that he had sent that girl to a deliberate death — he lived with that belief day and night — but, she wondered, did it ever really trouble him?

She rose on the thought, wanting to get to her bed and get warm. Intolerable weariness was back. As she moved from the settee, her foot struck against something and glancing down she saw Jerry's heavy gold cigarette case lying by her foot. She bent to pick it up and, forgetful that he had said he would be leaving first thing in the morning, she carried it up to her room with her.

CHAPTER THIRTEEN

THE following morning Fay awoke, unrefreshed, to the sound of a tea cup rattling in a saucer and the big, bosomy figure of the landlord's wife at the side of the bed. She struggled up out of the clinging embrace of the bed's huge feather mattress, trying to smile at the big woman who was smiling so pleasantly at her.

But she felt so ill.

And when the cup of strong tea was in her hand she felt even worse. She fought to combat the stupefying nausea, to reply to the woman.

"Now what would you like for breakfast?" the woman asked cheerily. "Haddock and egg? Bacon and egg? Or perhaps a nice pair of kippers?"

Fay shuddered, uncontrollably, at the mention of kippers and just about managed to murmur that toast was all she ate for breakfast. Toast would be fine.

"Toast?" The woman looked openly aghast. "Well, it isn't very filling, dearie. Are you sure?"

Fay nodded, desperate now with the need to be alone.

"All right, dearie, if that's what you'd like. Marmalade with it?"

"No — just toast."

"And the eggs are lovely this morning! Such a pity —"

"I'm — I'm not a very big eater," Fay murmured, longing to tell the kindly soul to take her enquiring eyes and all her talk of haddocks and kippers out of the room.

"Well, all right," the woman began to edge toward the door. "Nothing on the toast?"

Fay shook her head.

The door closed on the broad back and Fay sighed thankfully, before depositing the cup of almost orange tea on the bedside table. She lay back against the pillows and stared up at the sloping ceiling. She breathed deeply, slowly, fighting her nausea. She was close to tears. She felt so ill. She wanted Lew. She wanted his arms, to rest in them and be eased by them. . . .

The minutes slid by as she lay summoning the strength and courage to climb out of bed. She was shivering under the sheets.

Oh, this wouldn't do — this wouldn't do at all. She pushed back the covers, swung her legs over the side of the bed and forced herself to stand up. Her head swam, her knees almost buckled, and she knew a deadly fear, a fear that covered her back and her chest with a film of cold sweat.

She moved to the washstand and poured some of the hot water the landlord's wife had brought her into the china bowl. She forced herself to wash, to dress, to comb her hair. Then she dabbed her cold face with powder and applied a little lipstick with a shaking hand.

When she opened the door of the room and stepped out on to the landing, the stale smell of beer, rising from below, made her retch anew and clutch the side of the door. And as she clung there, feeling so wretchedly ill, fighting for the strength of will to go down to the bar parlor, where the sour smell of beer would be even stronger, the stout, yellow-overalled figure of the landlord's wife appeared at the head of the stairs.

Hurriedly she came along the landing, seeing Fay. "You're not well, dearie!" she exclaimed. She took hold of Fay and helped her back into the room, almost

128

carrying her to the bed. She leaned over her, her eyes enquiring and alarmed. "Anything I can do for you, dearie?" she asked.

Fay managed to smile at her. "Could you — wave a wand and conjure my husband?" she murmured.

"Can I phone him for you, love?" the woman asked at once.

Fay shook her head. "He's probably on his way here now," she said. "I'm — just being a little silly. I'll be all right in a while."

The woman was suddenly nodding and beaming, for she had tumbled to Fay's secret. Her red cheeks bunched up as she said. "The mornings always play you up, love. Why don't you rest yourself until this wears off? I'll bring your breakfast up to you, shall I?"

"You're very kind," Fay told her gratefully.

She managed to eat a slice of the toast the woman brought her, then she kicked off her shoes, rolled herself in the eiderdown on the bed and fell into a restless doze.

Many wavering images walked in that curious dream she began to have. Predominating, strangely enough, was the broad and earnest figure of Dr. Forrester. She could hear his slow, deliberate voice so plainly: "Are you afraid he won't want this baby? Is that your worry?" Then: "You'll be risking your child! You'll be risking your child!"

She turned restlessly, trying to lose the voice, the words. Who was he talking about? Who didn't want her baby? She tried to remember — she fought to remember. Someone must tell her! Who would tell her? Thalia? She went running along a white corridor that seemed to echo with voices, for she could see Thalia waiting at the end of the corridor, a strange, bizarre Thalia, who wore the white uniform of a nurse, but who still smoked a cigarette and smiled. "Who does he mean?" Fay demanded of her. "Tell me! Tell me! I must know!" She went to clutch hold of Thalia, but the white-clad Thalia moved like vapor out of her hands; she possessed no reality, she wavered and broke and eddied away, and Fay was alone in the corridor, with only the sound of the many voices coming in hollow waves to her ears.

She knew a stark fear. She began to run. She had to get away from this place. She sped along the white corridor, but the voices pursued her, a hollow baying, a dismal frightening symphony of sound, always at her heels. She saw a door and she made for it. She pushed at the door, but it wouldn't give, it wouldn't yield, it wouldn't open to let her in. She hammered and pounded on the door. She cried out: "Let me in! I don't want to stand out here! I'm frightened! These people frighten me! Let me in! Please let me in!"

But the door stayed shut, solid and immovable and Fay sank slowly down on the cold tiles of the floor. As her head drooped against the door, the voices behind her broke into a chorus of derisive laughter. She shuddered where she lay. She held her hands over her ears. "Let me in!" she beseeched. "Let me in before it's too late!"

But the door stayed shut.

And the dream faded and a kinder sleep came to her. A sleep empty of phantoms. When she awoke at last it was to the dark, watching face of Lew.

He was sitting beside her on the bed; as she opened her eyes and saw him, a deep thankfulness filled her. "Hullo!" she said, and her smile was soft and fond and full of peace. "Is it lunch time, or are you early?"

"I'm early," he replied, but he didn't return her smile. He watched her speculatively. He said, "The woman down in the bar told me you weren't feeling too good. She gave me a damned coy smile and a wink." He hesitated, just for a moment, then he went on curtly, "What am I supposed to do, Fay, guess the rest?"

"What — what do you mean?" She struggled into a sitting position, pushing the eiderdown back from her slender legs. She eyed him perplexedly. "Why are you vexed, Lew?" she asked.

His mouth thinned and his eyes swept down her, from her throat to her heels. "I wasn't born yesterday!" he snapped. "Presuming the kid's mine, why do I have to be left to learn about it from some publican's wife?"

"Presuming?" Fay stared at him, her blue eyes shadowed in her face. She watched him lean away from her and pick up something from the cane table beside the bed. He showed her the gold cigarette case she had put there last night, the gold case engraved with the intials J. K.

"Jerry's case!" she gasped, and all that was uppermost in her mind at that moment was that she had forgotten to give it to him.

"Does it reassure you, my dear? Does it bring back tender memories to have it by you while you sleep?" Lew enquired, his eyes glittering as they ranged over her face, with its sudden look of consternation. She gazed back at him, bewildered, unnerved. She couldn't make out what he was talking about. "I — I don't understand you, Lew," she said. "What's the matter?" She put a tentative hand on his arm, but he shook it off impatiently.

"I'm asking you what this cigarette case of Kaufmann's is doing here." His voice cut into her, making her flinch.

"He dropped it — last night —"

"He what?"

"He was here." She spoke quickly, eager to explain. "His car broke down and he had to put up here for the night."

"The devil he did!" Lew stood up, towered over her as she lay on the bed, among the rose-pink folds of the

131

eiderdown, gazing up at him like a bewildered child. "What a bit of luck for you, my dear," he sneered. "Did you make the most of your luck?"

"Oh, Lew!" The hurt tears, the tears that were all part of her physical weariness, her joy that he was back with her — her joy turned to bewilderment, flooded into her eyes. They spilled helplessly, rolling down her face. She turned her head from him. "What are you saying? Do you know what you're saying?" she whispered.

His answer was to throw the gold cigarette case down on the bed beside her. It hit the bed with a small, deadly thump. "There's your talisman, my pet," he said. "Pick it up, go on. It'll soothe your tears away."

But she withdrew from the case as from something repugnant. She was trembling violently. What made Lew so cruel? How was it possible she loved this man whose feelings were encased in armor? Whose pride was so overbearing that he burned at the thought that some other man might have cast proprietorial eyes over his flimsy toy; might, perhaps, have taken it into his hands for a moment?

He didn't love her, yet he exhibited this vicious jealousy!

Suddenly she was unutterably wearied of him — wearied of everything, even the effort of searching the cuff of her dress for her handkerchief, so that she might wipe away her tears. "Oh, think what you like, Lew!" she said and drearily fumbled her way off the bed — and fell forward into a bottomless void, falling, falling, but never quite reaching the bottom of that black pit, for strong hands caught her, lifted her and everything died in silence.

That afternoon, in a cottage hospital a mile or so outside of Thame, Fay lost her baby.

And Lew, in a torment he had never known before,

132

paced the waiting-room, cursing himself. Cursing his vicious temper that had made him say the things he had said to Fay. Suggesting — suggesting that Kaufmann. . . . The recollection made him sick.

He sank down on one of the tubular chairs in the waiting-room, running restless hands through his hair. God, what was happening? Why didn't the doctor come, or the nurse — anyone to tell him Fay was all right? Supposing she died! He sat in fear, staring at the red linoleum on the floor. He stared at the pattern until it seemed to dance into his brain, washing his brain in a red haze. The pitiful helplessness that had overtaken Fay in the bedroom of that pub was starkly painted. She had seemed to die as he had caught her, lifted her — all color fled from her face, all warmth from her body. She had gone floating away into realms where he could not follow, and he had known a stark fear, an unutterable sense of loneliness.

He had thought her dead.

God! Why didn't the doctor come? He rose and walked to the window and stood drumming his fingers on the cold glass, watching the slow fall of rain on the gnarled, barren limbs of the trees that stood in the darkening courtyard of the hospital.

It seemed hours to him before the door opened and the white-coated figure of the doctor entered. He came to say that Fay had lost her baby, that now she was sleeping and all Lew could do was take himself off until the morning.

"She is all right?" Lew's dark eyes were rather wild, and for all his height and breadth, he looked curiously young, almost boyish, to the doctor. "I mean, I'll stay the night if there's any danger of a relapse or — or anything."

"Good lord, no!" The doctor shook his head, smiling slightly. "Your wife will be able to talk to you in the morning. My advice to you right now is to go off and have a good meal and a good sleep." He banged Lew's shoulder cheerfully. "And stop worrying."

But Lew didn't stop worrying.

He was still worrying when he came back the next morning, following a pert young nurse into a small room where Fay lay in bed, her fair hair tied back with a piece of ribbon.

"Fifteen minutes, no more," the young nurse said. As the door closed on her, Lew moved to the foot of the bed, where Fay lay so quietly, all eyes and cheekbones and small, still hands on the taut sheet.

"I'm sorry about the baby, honey," he said huskily.

She watched him, thinking how dark, how big he looked in this white cubicle of a room, with its white-painted chest of drawers, its humming radiator. The acorn on the blind gently tap-tapped the window as the March wind outside filtered in through the open top of the window and stirred the blind.

She wondered why her heart didn't race in the old way, why the mere sight of him didn't quicken her pulse and gladden her eyes? She wondered why she felt so dead — so dead. It was as though all feeling, all emotion had been drained out of her, as though her heart had died with her baby.

"Why should you be sorry?" she asked, in a voice as devoid of emotion as she was. A cynical little smile moved in her eyes. "The baby was mine, wasn't it? God knows how I came by it on my own, but I must have, for I certainly didn't come by it in the way you implied yesterday."

He winced and his hands moved out to grip the rail of the bed. "You can't despise me more than I despise myself, Fay," he said, almost passionately. "I could kick myself for the things I said to you yesterday."

But her smile was tired, almost uninterested. "I wish I could despise you, Lew," she said. "Anything other than not being able to feel anything at all for you."

"What do you mean?" His hands clenched on the rail of the bed and his eyes stared down into hers. "What are you saying, Fay?"

"I'm looking at you, Lew, and I'm feeling absolutely nothing," she quietly replied.

He came round to her. He sat down in the chair that was beside the bed and he took hold of her left hand, lying so quietly on the coverlet. It felt very small and fine-boned in his hand.

"I don't blame you for feeling bitter, Fay, honey," he said. "I've a swinish, jealous temper and I say many things I should be shot for saying. But a bullet in the heart couldn't hurt me more than to hear you say you don't love me anymore."

"But, Lew, what's love?" she half smiled, echoing his own cynicism. "Stupid sentimentality, isn't it? A puff of air that is here one minute, gone the next? You were very right to say that. I loved you in the first hour I met you, but it's taken me just one day to stop loving you."

She ceased to speak, and he frowned, moving her hand, watching the beautiful wedding ring on it winking and glinting. His mind fled back to that day in the garden of his grandmother's house, Fay in her white uniform, asking: "How long will our marriage last, Lew? As long as this whim that's made you ask me?"

"Fay," he gripped her hand, "I can't lose you, my baby. I don't want to lose you. Won't you please believe me?"

She heard him. She wondered why she remained unmoved. She had often prayed for him to say these few words, and now that he had said them she felt nothing. No joy. No sweeping gladness.

"Fay," his eyes pleaded with her, "I won't let Kaufmann be the cause of a rift between us."

She shook her head tiredly on the pillow. "This has

nothing to do with Jerry — though he was the one who said that you had woven a spell about me. Now that spell has broken. I'm free! I want to stay free!" Now tears welled into her eyes and she turned her tired face from him. "Let me go! Let me go!" she whispered.

"Go where, baby?" He reached over and gently turned her face back toward him; he searched her face with dark, distressed eyes. "You can't mean you want to go away from me — you can't mean that, honey?"

"I do — I do!" Her head turned restlessly on the pillow, while tears slid silently and forlornly down her thin cheeks. "I shouldn't have come on this trip. The doctor warned me not to. I should have listened to him — I would at least have kept my baby if I had listened to him!"

The words broke on a sob and a spasm of pain went across Lew's face as he bent above her. "I can't make out why you didn't tell me about the baby, honey. All of this needn't have happened if you'd told me. Surely I was entitled to be told?"

"I didn't think you'd want it." She spoke the dreary truth, too tired and drained of feeling to care whether she hurt him or not.

But he was hurt. She saw the wry pain come into his eyes. "Thanks!" he said. "Your opinion of me continues to be a pretty poor one, doesn't it, Fay? What did you think I'd do to you — toss you out on your ear?" He spoke with a jocular grimness that would surely have moved her to remorse — yesterday. But yesterday she had loved him.

Her tears were suddenly spilling helplessly, and the young nurse, returning at that moment, came hurriedly to the bedside when she saw that Fay was crying. "You'd better go now, Mr. Marsh," she said quietly. "Your wife's still rather weak. She should be resting."

He nodded, gazing in impotent distress at Fay. The

things she had said had hurt terribly, but the way she looked at him, as though at a stranger, hurt even more. He could understand her bitterness — he had earned that. But her indifference hurt.

Then he leaned forward and gently kissed her cheek, feeling her tears salt against his lips. "We'll talk about all this tomorrow," he said. "You'll feel better about everything tomorrow." But her eyes, looking back at him through the raining, helpless tears, were as bleak and uncomprehending as the eyes of a lost child, and she made no answer to his murmured good-bye.

When he returned the following morning he found her restored to calmness. She even gave him a slight, if restrained smile, as he entered the room and came round to sit beside her, holding her small, passive hand.

"Honey, listen to me," he said. "Now that Brewster's agreed to do the film — I got him to agree, y'see," — his smile flashed for an instant, "we'll be going into production. The exterior scenes are going to be shot in Spain. Don't you want to come to Spain?"

She quietly shook her head.

He looked openly taken aback. "I can't make you out," he said, with a sudden touch of exasperation. "Spain's a beautiful country, exciting, romantic — you'd enjoy yourself. What will you find to do all alone in England?"

"I'm going back to my nursing," she replied.

Now the exasperation that had been in his voice spread to his face. His mouth grew thin. "Is this — this display of childishness because I said something to you in a fit of temper? I've apologized for that. What have I got to do, crawl on to my knees before you'll accept my apology?"

She half smiled. "No, Lew," she said. Her voice was

137

quiet and steady. Physically she was much better and this showed in her face. Her exhausted look was quite gone and her lips had some color. She looked perfectly calm and absolutely sure of what she wanted to do and why she wanted to do it. "I'm not showing off with you, or being childish, Lew. I've recovered my pride, that's all. I can't — I won't be your little Cinderella any more. Your little dressed-up doll! I won't be sent out to walk round the park, or be told what to wear, not anymore. I won't come running when you snap your fingers." Her eyes were steady on his face and entirely absent of any defiance. She spoke with the simplicity of complete and unalterable decision. "I won't come to Spain with you, Lew."

"You really mean to go back to your old life?" he exclaimed, incredulously.

She gave a firm little nod of her head. "I've always known I should have to sooner or later," she replied calmly. And then she did something that showed him how complete was her repudiation of him. She withdrew her hand from his, took off her wedding ring, and held it out to him. He sat staring at her, his dark face grim, his mouth granite hard. She gazed back at him, quite undismayed. She took hold of his hand, turned it palm upward, and dropped the ring into it, closing his fingers over the expensive glitter and the empty meaning of it.

Her eyes didn't show the exultation she was feeling, but it was running warmly, richly in her blood. She had pushed Lew out of her heart. She had closed the gates of her heart on him — on him, the insolent invader. She had regained pride and self-possession. She had won free of her enslavement.

She watched as his hand slowly clenched on the ring, she watched as the meaning of what she had done took hold of him.

"Aren't you afraid," he asked quietly, "that I'll make

138

you come to Spain with me? You're still my wife, remember?"

"I'm that, Lew, but I'm not your little dog on a lead," she retorted. "You can't make me go anywhere I don't want to go. You can't," she smiled, "you can't drag me along by my hair."

"Ah, but I know another way." His eyes were suddenly insolent. He smiled at her. He bent over her and quite gently, but with unmistakable possessiveness, kissed her mouth. She felt the familiar warmth and hardness of his mouth, she breathed the clean warmth of his skin, the aromatic scent of his cigars — she was totally unmoved by his kiss. It was as though a stranger kissed her.

When he lifted his head, she saw from his eyes that her cold and unemotional reception of his kiss had shaken him. He studied her serene face on the pillows, her eyes that no longer wavered from his in shy confusion or gazed back at him with something of fear moving in their blue depths.

"Love is a fickle jade, isn't she?" he drawled. "Or am I just unlucky in my choice of women?"

"Just unlucky, I guess, Lew." Then she patted his hand, the one that held her wedding ring. "Inez Holden didn't commit suicide, Lew. Did you know?"

"Yes, I knew." He smiled cynically. "She was too darned selfish to deliberately throw her beauty under a gasoline truck."

Fay winced at the words. Lew saw and abruptly he stood up, thrusting her wedding ring into his pocket. "All right, Fay," he said, "if you want me to go out of your life, I'll go."

CHAPTER FOURTEEN

So Lew went to Spain alone.

Fay saw him go without emotion. Emotion still seemed held in abeyance within her. She no longer cried, even for the baby she had sacrificed for Lew's sake. She felt isolated from the past, from all the feeling she had once known, where pain had mingled with ecstasy, where hate had touched hands with love.

Lew had rented a flat for her in London, but it came about that she occupied that flat for a bare three weeks after he left for Spain.

Still convalescent from her miscarriage and aware that it would be the height of foolishness for her to commence her nursing yet, she filled in her days with a little walking, a little reading, a little letter-writing. She didn't know many people to whom she could write, but it did occur to her to write and tell Max Forrester that she had lost her child. She had liked Max. He had been warm and friendly and sympathetic and she was now at the stage of her convalescence where she was wanting to talk to a friend, if only through the impersonal medium of letter-writing. She told Max that she intended going back to her nursing, and in his answering letter he made a suggestion. It both appealed to her and yet kept her restless and wakeful that same night.

For Max wrote in his letter:

I think that you would enjoy working at the Anita Hill Hospital, my dear. You know the hospital, I know, for you once told me that your husband's friend died there. Perhaps, if you've sad memories of the place, it wouldn't be a wise move; yet on the other hand I feel that your deep personal problem can only be fought to a satisfactory conclusion in the place where it had its commencement, Hollywood. So I say face your bogy and come back to Hollywood. It was here that your married life was lived, not in England, therefore it is here, you know, where you must search your heart and find out for certain that you're not throwing away something you really want.

Fay tossed restlessly that night, her sleepless eyes roving the dark corners of this strange bedroom in the heart of a London that had grown strangely alien. Was Max right? Was he?

She threw her arms across her eyes, trying to collect her racing thoughts into some semblance of order. The Anita Hill Hospital in Hollywood, white-stoned and terraced, with orange trees in the meticulously kept grounds and a very modern nurses' home not ten minutes' walk from the hospital buildings. The place where Bill Symans had quietly died.

Fay, after a while, drifted into sleep, and with the arrival of morning there also came decision. Face your bogy, Max had said; come back and search out your heart.

And so, her courage collected about her like a mantle, Fay returned to Hollywood, where Max Forrester used his influence to get her a post at the Anita Hill.

Fay had always been a good nurse and the familiar routine of a job she could do with great efficiency soon claimed her. The busy days grew into weeks and the weeks passed swiftly. Though Fay had decided upon her arrival to write and tell Lew that she was back in Hollywood, she found herself increasingly reluctant to put pen to paper. For after all — what did it matter?

Fay joined in the social life of the hospital very little, uninterested in tentative approaches from one or two young doctors who would have been pleased to take her out, aware that though she was married, she was at present living apart from her husband. She was strangely content with her own company in those days, going for long walks in her free time, occasionally calling in for a cup of coffee with Mimi Forrester, Max's wife. Then, one afternoon, seeing an old film of Jerry Kaufmann's advertised at a local cinema, she went in to see it. She sat in the perfumed darkness of the cinema, staring at the bright, noisy screen, where a Jerry she did not know played a hard-swearing G.I., at war in a steaming jungle, dying grotesquely upon the bayonet of a grinning Japanese soldier. Possibly a powerful piece of acting, she thought, rather dazedly — but this was not the cheerful warm Jerry she had known: the Jerry who had bought her enormous toffee apples and chased her along the warm silver sand of Pacific Beach. She rose blindly and made her way out of the cinema, memories crowding back, taking her dead heart back to pain. Dear, dear Jerry — where was he now?

May passed into June, and then, with the arrival of July, there came a spell of sultry, trying weather, with long days of almost tropical rain and an outbreak of a summer 'flu that filled the hospital to overflowing. Fay was therefore kept extremely busy, with no time for introspection. There was no time to search the heart Lew had come so close to breaking. It was with a startled surprise that she glanced at the calendar in the nurses' sitting room one morning and saw that August had arrived.

One of the other nurses, noticing Fay's absorption in

the calendar, remarked, "How quickly this year's going! This time last year I was on my holidays. My boyfriend and I pooled our resources and flew to Honolulu; we had a marvelous time!" She smiled warmly at Fay. "Recalling your own holidays, honey?"

"I wasn't on holiday," Fay's smile was fleeting. "I was nursing a very rich old lady, in Casa Roche. A Mrs. Laura Marsh, full of majesty and mustard and quite a character — you know."

"A Mrs. Laura Marsh — in Casa Roche?" The girl stared at Fay. "That's funny!" She darted to the table that stood in the middle of the nurses' sitting room and picked up the morning paper. She rapidly turned the pages, found what she was looking for, and brought the paper to Fay. "Read that, ducky," she said. "Might be your old girl — who knows!"

Fay quickly, rather nervously, scanned the item — and her heart turned cold. Oh yes, this was old Mrs. Marsh, whom she had nursed. Old Mrs. Marsh, tart of voice, quick of eye, full of love for Della, quite empty of feeling for Lew — and she was dead — found dead of a heart attack by her granddaughter!

The skin of Fay's face felt cold and taut. Della had found her grandmother: Della, that handsome, rather lost creature, who had depended so much on the love of that autocratic old lady. Fay's hand closed hard on the newspaper. Then, abruptly, she swung on her heel and hurried from the nurses' sitting room, making for the matron's office.

"You're asking for leave, when we're so busy?" Matron stared at her.

"Only three or four days, Matron. It's rather important."

"Well — I don't know." Matron tapped a pencil on the desk and thoughtfully regarded the small, earnest face confronting her across the desk. A good nurse, this one, and hard-working. . . . "Very well, you may

143

take your four days, nurse," she said abruptly. "I take it this is family business?"

"Yes, Matron."

Fay paid off the rather dilapidated taxi that had brought her to Laurel Bay and mounted the four wide steps to the front door. Her hand was reaching for the bell when the door swung open and the gangling, red-haired figure of Will Bronson stood before her. His green eyes were full of surprise. "I saw you from the window. Lord, Fay, it's good of you to have come." He ushered her into the dim, flagged hall. "Lew's here. He got here this morning."

"Lew!" Fay stared up at Will as they crossed the hall to the drawing room. "I — I didn't know he was back in America."

If this statement surprised Will, he didn't show his surprise, but as they paused before the door of the drawing room, he said, "Look, Fay if — if you and Lew are having a spot of marriage trouble, don't say anything to Dell about it. Lew hasn't. When Dell wanted to know why you hadn't come with him, he made the excuse that you had a bad cold and couldn't travel. You see — well, Dell isn't quite herself just now. She's having a baby and the shock of old Mrs. Marsh's death hasn't done her a lot of good."

"A baby!" Fay's hand reached for Will's arm and pressed it. "How nice for you!"

The grin he gave her was boyishly pleased. "Dell is hoping that the baby turns out to be a boy; but I'm more democratic, I'll take whatever comes."

"Della's pleased, then?"

"She was happy as a lark about the baby, but as I say, poor old Mrs. Marsh's death has rather put the damper on everything for her just now. They were very attached, you know — and Mrs. Marsh always seemed such a tough old girl."

144

He opened the door of the drawing room and Fay, small and braced, preceded him into the room. Nothing had changed. The massive mahogany furniture gleamed richly, the chandeliers glittered overhead and the heavy plum-colored curtains gracefully draped their silk skirts upon the silver-gray carpet. Fay crossed the room, aware of Lew rising from a deep armchair, watching her with dark startled eyes.

"Fay!" he said.

"Fay!" Della said.

And it was to Della Fay went, kneeling down beside the couch where she sat, wrapping soft arms about her. "Oh, Fay!" Della clung to her. "I'm so glad you came after all! So glad!" Then, the words barely out of her mouth, Della began to cry. She cried with the sudden hurt abandon of a child, gasping against Fay's shoulder. "I found her, Fay. Sh-she was dead in a ch-chair. I thought — I thought she was asleep. I loved her so . . . I loved her s-so!"

And during that storm of weeping, Will leaned impotently over the back of the couch, his red hair tumbling on to his forehead, his green eyes distressed. Lew remained as he had risen at Fay's entrance; standing outside this tableau of grief and sympathy, a hand slowly reaching into his pocket for his cigar case. He selected a cigar, carefully lit it, puffed the rich smoke in a blue cloud about his face, and through the cloud, he stared at Fay.

The funeral took place the following day and Della, having shed her bitter tears, was quite calm. It was at the reading of the will afterwards that she lost her calm. Mrs. Marsh had left all of her substantial fortune, which included valuable property holdings, and this house, Laurel Bay, to Della. Lew wasn't mentioned.

"But it isn't fair!" Della cried, jumping to her feet

145

and confronting the lawyer, her face flushed and dismayed. "Lew and I should share! I don't want the lot!"

Lew rose to his feet. He lazily approached Della and threw an arm about her, pulling her against his side. He smiled at the lawyer. "I'm perfectly happy with the will," he drawled. "I never expected to be in it."

"But Lew," Della turned to him, passionately, "it isn't fair! You're entitled to share with me."

"It's absolutely and utterly and completely fair," he elaborated, amusedly. "You were always the sun over the tall trees to old Gran, while I was always the bad boy in the corner, so it's perfectly reasonable, my honey, that she should leave you all her worldly possessions. Now stop getting yourself into a stew over it; do what Gran wants you to do. Bring Laurel Bay alive with half a dozen gingernuts." He winked at Will as he spoke. "I daresay Will will cooperate."

Della couldn't forget the will, however. She spoke to Fay about it after the lawyer had gone, taking hold of Fay's hand and walking her out to the garden. "I know Lew couldn't care less about the money part," she said, "but it was darned hurtful of Gran, all the same, to exclude him so completely. She never liked him, I know — but to do that!" Della's fingers suddenly tightened upon Fay's, then slowly she lifted Fay's hand and stared at it. "Where's your wedding ring, Fay?" she asked.

"My — wedding ring?" Fay bit her lip. "Why I —"

"You don't have to say," Della broke in. "You don't have to tell me."

"Don't I?" Fay withdrew her hand from Della's and turned almost embarrassedly to pluck a Michaelmas daisy from a nearby bush. She stood pulling it to bits. "I should never have married Lew, should I?" she said. "But I guess I was unutterably flattered that he should want me."

146

· "And now?" Della murmured. "Now what do you feel?"

Fay quietly considered the question, the little mauve petals of the Michaelmas daisy fluttering from her fingers. "I feel nothing. The magic is all gone and now I can think of him with composure. I never used to be able to, you know. Once he was the sun in the morning for me. The smell of tall trees with the rain on them; the fleeting glimpse of a star falling through the sky. He was everything magical and extraordinary — and then — then the magic died. It fizzled out, like short-circuited lights on a Christmas tree, and I was left gazing at nothing."

"Nothing!" Della echoed. "How sad that sounds."

Fay shrugged her shoulders and tossed the denuded heart of the little daisy from her. She turned to Della and took hold of her hands. "Now listen, Dell," she said, "you're not to worry about Lew and me. It's best we part."

"But why — why?"

"Because, my dear, a marriage, like a house, won't stand erect on one wall. I tried for seven months to make it do that, but the inevitable collapse came in the end. Now I've no desire to rebuild on the ruins."

"Has Lew — has he asked you to rebuild?" Della's dark eyes were curiously wistful as they held Fay's.

Fay shook her head. "I don't want him to, Dell. I just don't want him to." Then she squeezed Della's hands. "How about you and Will? Are you happy with him, my dear?"

"Oh, yes — he's awfully good to me. So — so patient and kind."

"He'll make a splendid father."

"So would Lew — don't you think?" Della spoke with a little rush. "I — I mean, men who haven't been all that happy themselves as children, well, they usually ensure that their own children have a good time."

147

"Wasn't Lew happy as a boy?" Fay asked — and in her mind's eye she saw Lew as a boy; tall and imperious, doing all the wrong things and only laughing when he did them; too much like his beautiful Sicilian mother for his grandmother to have any affection for him.

"Lew was kind of wild, you see," Della said. "Old Gran never really understood him, I guess she took more to me because I was younger, more able to adapt myself to her ways. Did you know that Lew worshipped our mother?"

"No!" Fay's blue eyes flew wide open. "No, I didn't know that. I received the impression that he actually hated her."

"He did after she remarried and walked out on us. He was twelve, you see; he was of an age to be terribly hurt by something like that. It hardened him; kind of killed all his faith in women; instilled a perpetual mistrust. I — I know he must have hurt you, Fay, for you to want to cut free of him, but don't hate him."

"I don't hate him, Dell." Fay replied quietly.

It was at dinner that evening that Lew said to Fay, "Dell tells me you've got to get back to your hospital on Thursday. I've some business to attend to in Hollywood, so why don't we travel together?"

But before Fay could answer him, Della broke in, "Say darn to that old hospital and stay here for good! Go on, Fay!"

Fay gave a little laugh, while Lew's expressive left eyebrow quirked amusedly. She saw no active objection to Lew's suggestion that he travel back with her. It was true she shied a little from the thought that the intimacy of a train journey together might induce more personal conversation than that they had yet indulged in since meeting again, yet she also felt that she'd be equal to it. Lew no longer frightened her; she found him little changed outwardly, yet there was a quietness about his eyes, a lack of boldness in his glance, that told her he had changed. He had changed, she thought, in that he had come to accept the fact that she was no longer his, over whom he could cast that sweeping, imperial glance of old.

"I quite like working at the Anita Hill," Fay said. Then she glanced at Lew. "Are you sure you have to leave on Thursday? I shan't be dragging you away, shall I?"

"Lord, no!" He chuckled. "Dell will be glad to see the back of me."

Della pulled a face at him. "That isn't true and well you know it, Lew Marsh. I'd like you to stay for good as well, except that you'd be rather a dangerous influence on my nice Will."

Her nice Will, who was carefully removing brazils from their shells and putting the nuts on Della's plate, shot his lopsided grin at her. "Eat your nuts and stop insulting me. I was quite a lady-killer before you hooked me."

Della took a nut and obediently chewed it, her eyes upon the glistening bronze of Will's hair. "I'm wondering whether I shall enjoy having a red-haired baby," she said. She smiled at Fay. "If my son dares to be born with red hair, I'll give him to you, Fay. With your craze for babies, you wouldn't care a darn about the color of his hair, would you?"

"Not a darn," Fay returned lightly — unaware that Lew was staring at her. "Anyway, my dear, your baby will probably be born with a head as smooth and hairless as a billiard ball — had you thought of that?"

When Fay, accompanied by Lew, took her departure from Laurel Bay, a slight mist was hanging over the house, blurring its friendly lights as the cab shot down the drive.

The mist seemed thicker in the country lanes, and

by the time they reached the railway station it was beginning to bank into a gray-yellow fog. Lew glanced at his wrist-watch as they stood on the platform, awaiting their train. "This murk is delaying our train," he remarked.

"Have you an appointment in Hollywood, then, Lew?" Fay asked.

"It's nothing that won't keep. Just a preliminary consultation about the European showing of *Lucrece*."

"*Lucrece?*" Fay smiled slightly.

Lew joined her smile. "Karl has decided that the full title is a bit much, so we've cut it down."

"Is it a good film, Lew?"

"I think so. The exterior scenes are great. You'd have loved it in Toledo, Fay, where we shot some of the film."

She didn't answer, and he went on: "It's a strange place; it stirs the blood with its old, wild secrets and its tall, shuttered houses, built from rock. It's a place that hasn't changed in centuries."

And then they heard their train, felt the speeding tremble of it under their feet as it bore down upon them. It rushed to a clamorous standstill, a monstrous thing, pulsing with power and belching white steam into the eddies of fog drifting along the line.

They entered a compartment and Fay sank down into a corner seat. Suddenly, right out of the blue, she found herself saying, "Tell me, Lew, whatever did you do about Jerry Kaufmann's cigarette case? It was rather expensive and I shouldn't like to think that it got lost."

Lew was tossing their overnight cases to the luggage rack and he glanced around at her in some surprise. "You haven't seen him since?" he exclaimed.

"Why, no!" She sat down, drawing off her gloves and tucking them into the flap at the back of her handbag — in the old neat way Lew remembered so well.

150

"No, I haven't seen Jerry." Then she smiled slightly. "That is I did see a film of his some time ago, but I haven't seen him to speak to."

"I — see." Lew sat down facing her, swinging one long leg across the other, pulling the impeccable crease back into the knee of his crossed leg — in the way Fay remembered so well. "I left the cigarette case with the landlord of the pub," he said curtly. "I wasn't going to put myself out, returning that guy's damn property."

"That was a pretty miserable quarrel we had over that cigarette case, wasn't it, Lew?" Fay met his eyes, briefly, remembering that quarrel, all that it had led to. Then she glanced away from him, gazing out at the slow drift of fog past the windows of the train, listening idly to the slamming doors along the train. It was stirring back into powerful life now, a waking giant, protesting with loud belches of steam as it began to move away from the platform, gathering momentum every second, plunging forward into the fog.

"Miserable, my dear?" Lew said, drawing her eyes back to his face, grown darker than ever from the hot sun of Spain, a chiselled mask, out of which the dark eyes glowed with a sudden passion she couldn't fathom. "Monstrous is a better word, I think! You've every reason to hate me. I haven't forgotten the things I said to you. I haven't forgotten that I struck your baby dead with my brutal tongue."

"Don't!" She threw out a hand, as though to ward off his words, the memories they evoked. "Don't, Lew! That's all over, all finished. Don't let's talk about — about the baby."

"No — perhaps you're right." He laid his head back against the dark plush of the train seat, the action strangely melancholy, strangely tired. "Well, how's nursing, Fay? Are you happy at the Anita Hill?"

"Very happy," she said.

"I'm glad. I want you to be happy." His eyes moved over the delicate contours of her face, took in the new way she was wearing her hair. Gone was the soft page-boy of their married days, now her hair was cut almost boyishly short. She looked, he thought, jaunty and independent — and so pretty! "I couldn't believe my eyes when you walked into Laurel Bay the other day, my dear," he said. "I thought you were still in England."

"I meant to write and tell you that I was back in Hollywood, but we've been kept so busy at the hospital." She shrugged slightly. "There never seemed to be time for writing letters —"

"I quite understand, Fay." His lips quirked on a ghost of his old derisive grin.

"There seemed no point, Lew." She met his eyes with a candid frankness. "We had said everything — what could I add?"

"Do you really think we've said everything?" Abruptly he leaned towards her, his face grown a little grim, his eyes intent upon hers. "Where do we go from here, Fay? Do you want me to divorce you?"

Fay looked up at him curiously for a moment, then sighed wearily. "It makes very little difference to me. Is that what you want?"

"I, surprisingly enough, want whatever you want," he returned quietly. Then he added, "I take it we go on as we are now? We continue as polite strangers?"

"Perhaps it is the best way." She held out a hand appealingly, and for a moment it seemed as if he would take that out-thrown hand, then his own half-raised hand fell back to his knee. He sank back in his seat, watched her broodingly for a second or two. "You really are happy?" he questioned again. "You're not lonely in Hollywood?"

She shook her head. "I'm not lonely. I have two very

152

nice friends — Mimi and Max Forrester. You don't have to worry about me, Lew. Or feel that I'm a distant responsibility — I don't want that."

"Not that, nor me!" The smile he smiled then was wholly cynical. "Well, I'm not blaming you. You're wise to clear your house of rubbish."

"Oh, Lew!" She had to laugh — yet it was a laughter that rose on a rather wobbly note, as though he moved her, despite herself. "Lew," her blue eyes were very earnest, gazing across into his, "let's get one thing straight, at least. I — I don't hate you, just because I no longer — well, I don't hate you I don't!"

"Methinks you insist too earnestly," he broke in, looking sardonic.

"Lew, I must make you understand." She passed her hand across her head in a worried gesture, ruffling the shining hair, making it stand up, unaware of how endearing that lapse from neatness made her look to him. "Love — love made of me a creature without a shell, something that got wounded so easily. Love stripped everything from me — independence — protection. But freedom from love has restored my shell and I don't get hurt any more." Her chin lifted and her eyes held purpose. "I'm safe now — and happy."

Safe! Happy! Free!

The wheels of the hurrying train took the words and they became one with the rhythm of the train. Lew heard them and knew a wild need to escape them. Fay — no longer wanting love, shrinking from it, she who was so made for love! He rose blindly to his feet. "I'm going out to the corridor to smoke." He spoke hurriedly, harshly, already moving past her to the door. "Do you mind?"

She shook her head, watching him as he stepped out into the swaying corridor and strode from her sight.

CHAPTER FIFTEEN

LEW smoked moodily, staring into the hazy darkness beyond the corridor window and seeing only the darkness of his own thoughts.

So the dreary emptiness of the past four months was to go on — because he had stooped low enough to believe that Fay, gentle, compassionate Fay, with her flower-like sweetness could betray him as Inez Holden had betrayed him.

Inez — he'd nearly choked the life out of her that night she had come to him and laid claim to still loving him. His angry hands had closed about her throat, but gazing down at her face, so flawlessly beautiful, yet now, to him, only a lying mask covering a cheap recklessness, a weary disgust had replaced his anger. His fingers had caught in the pearls about her throat, the pearls that had been his engagement present to her. As the string had broken and the lovely, iridescent things had rained to the carpet like tears, he had contemptuously marched her to the door and put her out of his life.

With the slam of the door he had sworn that never again would a pair of blue eyes get under his skin; never again would any woman be more to him than a means of pleasure.

And he had kept that promise — kept it so well that now he had lost the best thing that had ever come into his life, he had lost Fay's love.

Fay's love! Small, melting body in his arms; lovely mouth flaming into a rose under his mouth.

Fay's love, which he had killed; which he had struck dead with that unutterable insinuation that Jerry Kaufmann had fathered her baby, and so many other hurtful blows through the months. Lew shied from the memory; from the terrible hurt that had been in Fay's eyes.

Half an hour later, when he rejoined Fay, he found her still sitting quietly in her corner, her eyes turned toward the window. She didn't seem to hear him and he stood watching her from the doorway of the compartment, swaying to the motion of the train.

And then, like a heart missing a beat, the rhythm of the train seemed to change. A faltering shudder seemed to pass along the entire length of it, to be present under the wheels, in the body of it, and then overhead. It came like a flick of lightning, and Fay, in that moment, did glance up — to see Lew, in whom the instinct of danger was as primitive and as lively as his quick tempers and his quick passions, diving across the compartment towards her, reaching for her with his powerful arms. Covering her body with his body as the train, in that split second, went hurtling off the lines and the whole world became one long, hideous scream of wrenching metal, rending wood and splintering, hailing glass.

Darkness swept down like a black wing; a spinning eternity of darkness, in which was held, it seemed forever, the high and terrible keening of people in sudden agonizing pain and terror.

And then — and then, as fear pierced through the paralysis of numbing horror that the initial impact, the first moment of shock induced, Fay cried out against the nightmare, fighting to breathe, to ease her lungs of the lifeless weight that seemed to be crushing them, while somewhere in the dark, terrible night a pandemonium of dark, terrible noise was raging — a noise that surely belonged in bedlam or in hell!

She couldn't see. She could only feel — feel her aching, stunned body — feel incredulous disbelief. It chased round and round in her head, a panic-stricken voice crying out an unending stream of jumbled words. "We've crashed!" "I must have my freedom — I must — I must!" "We've crashed!" "We've crashed!" Round and round.

She moved, she pushed with her hands at the weight that lay so heavily upon her, numbing her, stifling her. She felt that weight give a little and it was warm to her hands — she felt with her hands the material of Lew's jacket. She remembered — she lived again that moment when she had glanced up to see him diving across the compartment toward her, his dark face alive with purpose in that deadly moment of his awareness that the train stood on the brink of disaster. His eyes nakedly revealing his determination to reach her before the racking moment of shock and horror came. She had read something in them that lying stricken, barely able to breathe, she had neither the sense nor the will to truly comprehend. She couldn't think of it now. Very possibly she had dreamed what she had seen, but she couldn't think of it now!

She struggled to release herself from the dead weight of Lew's body. If only — if only she were able to see! It was so dark, everything was so dark! Then her hands came free and she held Lew while she slowly pulled herself from beneath him. She lay in splintered wood and glass, panting with the effort she had made, her throat dry and harsh with dust and the hot, metallic tang of fumes that threw a pall over everything.

Having regained a little breath, she felt again for Lew. She could hear the hoarse, shallow drag of his breathing. As she felt impotently about him, praying for a lift in the darkness so that she might see how

156

badly he was hurt, the sudden lurid flare of a fire sprang up outside, bathing the shambles that had been this compartment in red, flickering light.

Fay knelt by Lew, pushing at the rubble that lay over him, pushing it from his back and his sides — her hand coming away wet as she touched the left side of him. She saw, by the high, dancing light of the fire outside, that he lay at a curious angle. The right side of his body, from where she had crawled, lay free of impediment, but when she carefully felt along the left side of him, where that ominous wetness was rapidly spreading, she found that his arm was pinned. It was thrown forward, as though he had attempted to ward off the onrush of disaster; pinned just above the elbow, gripped in the jaws of something unyielding and metallic, that refused to give an inch to her exploring, suddenly wrenching fingers.

Blood was soaking the material of Lew's jacket, flooding out on the rubble where he lay, and Fay, realizing the futility of trying to release the arm on her own, turned with abrupt calmness to the task of stemming that terrible flow of blood.

With the quick, sure hands of her profession, she untied Lew's tie, sought in his breast pocket for the silver pencil and the pocket-knife he always carried there. Finding them, she rapidly ripped with the knife at the material of his left sleeve, ripped it away from the upper part of his arm, ripped away as well the linen of his shirt, baring the arm so that she might apply a tourniquet. Though deadly fear was in her, a cold, numbing fear that turned her sick and ill, she worked with steady, controlled hands.

She tore away the skirt of her slip for the improvising of a pad, rolling it as firmly and thickly as she could, applying it to the main artery of the arm and then encircling the arm with the silk tie, placing it firmly over the centre of the pad. Then she crossed the silk in a half-knot at the other side of the arm, laid the slim silver pencil against the half-knot and tied a reef knot, twisting the pencil to tighten the silk tie against the pad, twisting fiercely, exerting all her strength, fighting to stay that red flood.

The tie tightened around the arm, and Fay knelt there like a small Valkyrie, her fair hair in wild disorder, her face smudged with blood and dirt, her ears pierced by the indescribable tumult that raged outside.

People were running backward and forward in nightmare hysteria, calling out. Above it all suddenly raged the clarion call of racing ambulances, the hellish wailing of police-car sirens, the pealing of fire bells. But Fay felt outside of it all, alone on an isle of distress with Lew. The pain of others meant nothing to her. She was only concerned with bringing aid to Lew, stripped of all pretence forever, her very soul flaring with passionate thankfulness as she saw that her crude tourniquet was doing its work and that the life blood was ceasing to pump from Lew's veins.

She knotted the silk tie and though her heart was pounding so hard it was shaking her body, her hands did not shake. Now she must bring help from outside. Now she must bring a doctor.

She left Lew. She scrambled from the compartment window, where the glass had shattered into a thousand fragments, uncaring of the small, jagged pieces that remained in the edges of the frame, tearing her legs and her arms as she forced her slender body out onto the railway line. She ran along the line, pushing past the dazed forms of people, who, like herself, had escaped injury. She pushed past those who searched either frantically or with dread hopelessness in the fallen train for friends and relatives.

Fire and fog and screaming jets of steam seethed above the broken monster body of the train and Fay ran through the haze like a small ghost — shying once, and averting her eyes from scenes of horror.

Then Fay saw the white-coated figure of a doctor bent above a stretcher on the line. Half stumbling, breathless with the acute need to bring aid to Lew, she made straight for him. He had a couple of ambulance men with him and when Fay reached the group, as though in answer to her wild prayers, the men bore away the stretcher. She gripped the doctor's arm. "Will you come?" she implored. "There's someone — he's trapped! Will you come?"

The face lifted to his in the white light of the arc lamps was desperate in its urgency, and he said not a word, only turning to follow her. Her urgency carried to him — to him, to whom death was but an incident. Something that happened five days out of seven. The terrible pitifulness and tragedy of all this was borne home to him by the very way this girl hurried to combat death, to push back death from someone she loved.

When they reached the place where Lew lay, the white light of the lamps had replaced the red glare of the fire. Fay crawled in through the window, the doctor following her. They knelt in the rubble beside the trapped, unconscious figure of Lew and the doctor was brisk, examining the tourniquet Fay had applied.

"Not bad, at a moment's notice," he said. "It's a lucky thing for him you knew how to do this."

"I'm a nurse," she replied quietly, watching Lew's still profile resting in the dust and rubble. She could see the black mark of a bruise on his temple; she could hear the labored drag of his breathing.

She watched as the young doctor sought with firm, knowledgeable hands for some sign of life in that mangled arm, entrapped so firmly in metal. And even before he turned a regretful face to her, she knew what he would say. "The arm's finished," he said. "As far as I can make out, the hand's severed at the wrist and the forearm's completely crushed." He spoke to her quite dispassionately, though he knew that this man meant all the world to her; it was written plain on her face and in her eyes. "I'll have to amputate. It would be pointless trying to release a perfectly useless arm." He watched her. He said carefully, "Will you help me?"

Fay always thought afterward that the calmness with which she assisted this doctor was heaven-sent. It had to be a gift from God, for she was as controlled as though she were assisting a surgeon in the clinical impersonality of an operating theatre. She was as controlled as though this man, over whose body she and this doctor worked, was a complete stranger.

The agony she was feeling didn't show — the terrible torment of heart and soul was clamped down tight inside her. She made no sound as he, who had been so physically perfect, was put among the ranks of the crippled and the maimed.

Then the doctor, his work swiftly and skillfully completed, hurried away to fetch ambulance men, and Lew lay lax and still, his breathing less ragged than it had been, for the state of unconsciousness he lay in had been intensified to a deeper state by chloroform.

Fay held him gently, stroking the black hair back off his forehead, beaded with a fine, cold sweat. And though her legs were cramped and cut from kneeling in splinters of wood and glass, her dress stiff and sticky with blood, her head pounding from the noise that continued to rage outside, she would have held him like this through eternity.

He had subjected his body to this torment for her sake — he had taken that dive across the compartment in order to spare her the tear of wrenching metal. He had shielded her; his eyes had held, nakedly, the wish to shield her — or die with her.

The ambulance men came and Lew was carefully

lifted from the wreckage, laid on a stretcher and borne away to an ambulance, where the young doctor who had performed the amputation immediately set about matching Lew's blood and starting a transfusion. Then he smiled reassuringly at Fay, leaped from the ambulance and swiftly closed the door. The ambulance then swung away from the nightmare, the tumult and the misery and flew through the night toward one of the hospitals that was receiving the injured and the dying from the train wreck at Farmer's Corner.

CHAPTER SIXTEEN

THE ambulance drew to a standstill in the rear entrance of the hospital and the men came round to carefully lift down Lew's stretcher. Fay followed dazedly as the stretcher was borne in through the doors of the hospital and swiftly transferred to a trolley. Fay watched as the blue and white clad figure of a Sister approached the trolley and spoke to the ambulance men.

Reaction was setting in now, and Fay stood swaying in the clinical brightness of the receiving-room, the odor of drugs stinging her nostrils, the murmur of many voices coming in sing-song waves to her ears. She fought off her weakness, pulled together the remaining shreds of her strength and her self-control as she moved toward the Sister, bent above Lew, lying so terribly still. Lew — with maimed strength! That magnificent vigor, that was like lightning flashing high above tall trees, stilled and stricken!

She forced her trembling knees to carry her through the mill of people — shock cases — men and women with bleeding faces and torn clothing — men and women who waited, as she waited, for a favorable verdict on someone they loved.

She stood by the trolley and listened as one of the ambulance men gave the Sister a rapid account of Lew's amputation. She heard the name, Dr. Ransome, and she vaguely realized that the name referred to that quiet, skilfully working person who had knelt with her in that shattered compartment and removed

Lew's arm, ligatured what remained with firm rapidity and smiled briefly, reassuringly at her when it was all over.

When the ambulance man ceased to speak, the Sister turned at once to her desk and took up the phone. Fay heard her ask for surgery. "I'm admitting an amputation," she spoke swiftly, her sympathetic gray eyes resting on Fay, who was mutely gazing down at the unconscious face of Lew, chalky under the tan and beaded with the fine sweat of shock. "Left arm," the Sister said. "Yes, I'm sending him up right away."

No time was wasted then, the usual preliminary of taking the trolley into a cubicle and calling a doctor to make an examination dispensed with. The trolley was wheeled rapidly from the receiving-room, the white doors swinging on it, and Fay turned from watching the doors, mechanically giving the Sister the particulars she asked for, Lew's name, age, address — wondering how she kept upright, wondering how her knees held her.

The Sister eyed her concernedly. "Are you all right?" she asked. "You've not been hurt yourself, have you?"

Fay shook her head. "I'm — I'm only shaken up. I'll be all right."

"Well, find yourself a seat," the Sister said. "I'll let you know how your husband's doing just as soon as I can."

"Thank you." Fay turned wearily from the desk and made her way across the room to where a few chairs remained unoccupied. She sank down into one of them, clasping her hands tightly together in an attempt to stop them from trembling.

"Dear God," she prayed, "don't let Lew die! Please, don't let that happen! He's borne enough tonight; don't take away all his splendid strength! Please — please!"

"Hullo there!" a quiet voice said.

She glanced up. She stared uncomprehendingly at the thin, serious face, the quiet eyes of Dr. Ransome, who had just arrived with one of the ambulances. She attempted a smile that merely moved her mouth a little.

"Don't go worrying yourself sick," he urged. "That young man is as tough as a tree. He'll pull through."

"He's — my husband." Her eyes were infinitely tragic in that moment. She was remembering, she couldn't stop remembering, that in the train, only a matter of half-an-hour before the crash, she had exultantly informed Lew that her happiness lay in being free of him. "He's my husband," she said again.

The doctor abruptly sat down beside her. "You've nowhere to go tonight, have you?" His eyes were steady on her wan face. "Would you care to put up at my sister's? She only lives a few blocks from here. She won't mind a bit having you."

"But I want to stay here!" She eyed him rather wildly. "I want to be near Lew. He might die."

"He isn't going to die." Dr. Ransome took hold of her cold, shaking hands, gripping them, trying to instill into them some of his own warmth and steadiness. "Where's all that wonderful courage of yours gone to?" he demanded. "Don't buckle under now. You fought most of your husband's battle down in that wreck, now we'll proceed with the rest. We won't let him die. I promise you."

"But I must stay here until I know — until I know!" she insisted. "I can't — I won't go until then."

"All right. Anyway, I'll give you my sister's address." He took a notebook and a pencil from his pocket and scribbled the address, tearing the leaf from the book and handing it to her. He smiled. "I hope you can understand my writing. Now I promise you Kate won't mind having you. She's used to the occasional strays I send along to her. She's an awfully good sort and I know you'll like her."

Fay held the piece of paper and it fluttered slightly, in time with her trembling. "You're an awfully good sort yourself," she told him gratefully.

He looked a trifle abashed. "Now what about money?" he asked quickly. "You'll need some for the cab." He took out his wallet and extracted a five-dollar bill, pressing it into her hand. "You don't mind taking money from a — a friend, do you?" he queried, his smile a little diffident.

She shook her head.

"Good!" He jumped to his feet. "You'll be fine with Kate. You'll be better with her than hanging about here all night."

She nodded. He was right of course. She would go to his sister's when someone came to say that Lew was going to be all right.

"Doctor," she gazed up at him pleadingly, "can't I help? Can't I do something? If I sit here, just thinking, I'll go crazy."

He hesitated. "You're hardly in a state —"

"Please!" She stood up. "Surely there's something I can do?"

"All right, perhaps you would be better doing something." He took hold of her arm and led her to the Sister's desk, where people were now milling excitedly, shouting questions and bringing a look of harassment to the gray eyes of the Sister as she tried to speak on the phone. "Please be quiet," she cried out to them. "We'll manage so much the better if you'll all try to be calm."

Then she saw Dr. Ransome leaning forward across her desk and she put her hand over the mouthpiece of the phone, eyeing him enquiringly. "I've found you a volunteer, Sister," he said. "This young woman is going to help with some bandaging. Okay?"

She nodded. "If you say so, Doctor. Does she know how to?"

His smile at Fay was gently amused. "Best hand at a bandage I ever saw," he retorted. He then conducted Fay to the ward that was being used this night as an emergency station.

Two hours later Fay stepped from a taxi outside Kate Ransome's house and pressed the doorbell with a tentative hand. Though Dr. Ransome had assured her his sister wouldn't mind putting her up for the night, Fay couldn't help feeling a bit of an intruder.

But Kate Ransome accepted her arrival with an unquestioning calmness that put Fay at her ease right away. She was very like her brother to look at. She was a little older, but she had the same serious sort of face that looked rather melancholy until it abruptly broke into a smile. And the way she drew Fay into the small, square hall, without fuss, merely nodding a calm head when Fay murmured that Dr. Ransome had sent her, revealed how well used she was to receiving into her home her brother's occasional "strays".

Her rapid appraisal took in Fay's torn and bloody clothes and she said. "You're from that wreck at Farmer's Corner, I can see. I was expecting David to send along some poor devil or other." She smiled and her smile warmed away all the serious reserve of her face. "I expect you could do with a bath, couldn't you?" she asked.

"Oh, I could indeed!" Fay exclaimed gratefully. "I feel in an awful mess."

As they mounted the stairs to the bathroom, Kate Ransome said, "Have you someone at the hospital?"

"My husband," Fay spoke quietly. "He's pretty bad, but he's going — he's going to pull through." Suddenly her eyes were swimming in tears. She leaned against the banister, abruptly giving way, relaxing her hold on the tears she had almost shed at Lew's quiet bedside.

She had been in the midst of bandaging a cut knee when a nurse had come to her and murmured in her ear that she could come up now and see her husband. The process of helping, of occupying her mind with a job she knew so well, had restored to Fay a measure of calm, but as she went with the nurse, hurrying along the white corridor and up the iron staircase that made her footsteps ring hollowly, all the pain, the anguish, had come flooding back.

She had stood at Lew's bedside, with its smell of ether and its suspended transfusion bottle giving back the life that had flowed out so freely between her fingers as she had worked to stem it with the crude aid of a silk tie and a silver pencil. Mingled with her prayer of thankfulness that he wasn't going to die was a terrible despair because she could never recall her words to him just before the crash. She had, with those words, put out of her life the only man she had ever wanted in it. She had told Lew that only in being free of him could she ever find happiness.

She bent to kiss him, touching his cheek with lips that trembled. His face on the pillow was withdrawn into deep sleep, and it broke her heart to see him — the strong, the indomitable — lying so helpless.

The nurse who had brought her to him said quietly, her eyes on the chiselled face, the black hair clinging wetly to the strong, wide forehead. "What a pity about his arm. He's such a fine-looking man, isn't he?"

Fay could only nod her head, she didn't trust herself to speak. She was clinging to her self-control with all her might. Lew had lost his strength for a while and she mustn't lose hers. He would need her, turn to her in the next few weeks, and she mustn't fail him, she mustn't be weak and silly.

But she cried now, in Kate Ransome's house, the salt and painful tears raining down her face, devoured by a pain so stark, so overwhelming, that even the wild shedding of tears did nothing to relieve it. If she and Lew had no future together, her pain-torn heart cried out, why, oh, why, had God not seen fit to kill her?

"I — I shouldn't be crying," she sobbed. "I really shouldn't. Lew's going to get well — so I shouldn't be crying."

Kate Ransome wrapped a warm arm of sympathy about her shoulders. "You cry just as much as you want to," she declared stoutly. "What did the good Lord give us tears for? They're in us to be shed on occasions like this. You go ahead and cry my dear."

CHAPTER SEVENTEEN

SOME weeks later Lew sat on the veranda of the hospital, a rug across his knees, sunshine in his eyes and an indulgent smile playing about his mouth as the slim, brunette nurse, Joyce, once again found an excuse to come out to him. She had brought, this time, a tall glass of iced orange juice.

"Are you sure you're not too far out in the sun?" she asked, fussing round him, straightening his rug and eyeing him with such an openly affectionate and maternal concern that he longed to burst into laughter. He wouldn't though, because, despite this grand passion she seemed to have developed for him, she was a nice kid and a grand nurse. They were all grand, these nurses, even though they did make him feel a bit like a sheik with a particularly adoring harem.

"I'll tell you what," he said, "you can bring me a hairbrush." He grinned at her. "I'd like to pretty myself up before my wife gets here."

She obligingly fetched him the hairbrush and stood watching him as he tidied his black hair. She thought him perfectly wonderful and she was dreadfully jealous of Fay. She could never bring herself to greet Fay with very much enthusiasm and she didn't now, hearing the quick, light steps in the room behind and seeing her step out on to the veranda.

"Good afternoon, Mrs. Marsh," she said stiffly, and went her way with a starched rustle of skirts.

Fay was obliged to smile as she approached Lew.

"I'm dreadfully sorry for that poor girl," she said. "She really has got it bad. You're a menace, Lew. You were bad enough with two arms, but you're far worse with only one."

She leaned against the rail of the veranda, slender and very fair in a cool navy blue suit with a crisp white collar. Her delicately arched feet were encased in mere wisps of navy suede.

"You're beginning to look much better, Lew," she said. It was true. Though his face still wore something of the look of the invalid, gone was that frightening chalky look under the tan; gone, too, that fine-drawn look around the eyes. He had, she thought, recovered from that terrible injury with remarkable rapidity — probably because he possessed such superb health and such nerves of steel. And these afternoons in the sunshine were doing him good.

Her eyes settled on his pinned sleeve, and the familiar stab of pitying regret took her heart. He had taken the loss of his arm with far more coolness than she had. She would never, she knew, forget that morning following the accident, sitting beside his bed in a borrowed dress of Kate Ransome's, waiting for him to wake and speak to her.

And his first words to her, as he slowly rose up out of the well of stupor that had held him for so many hours, had been, "I've got — the darnedest sensation — like — like being on a raft." His eyes, misty with pain and drugs, gazed straight up into hers. "Are you — all right?" he asked.

She nodded. She couldn't speak, her throat was hurting her too much. She wanted to throw herself down beside the bed, to bury her face in the covers and howl like a baby.

"Why — why am I here?" he asked. "What the devil am I — doing here?" She watched his eyes travelling round the room. She saw the perplexity in his eyes, the effort to remember, the effort to break through the drug-induced veil. His eyes slowly turned towards his left side, where the pain he was aware of, distant yet distinct, unreal yet real, was localized. Fay saw, then, that he was remembering — that the veil was shimmering to let him through.

His eyes returned to her colorless face. His eyes searched her eyes, read in them the awful truth. "They've taken off — my damned arm!" he gasped. He lay assimilating the dreary fact, and Fay, her heart torn in two for him, sat like stone, barely breathing. She waited, she watched — she saw his lips move and she bent her head to catch what he said. "Well, it could — it could have been my head," was what he said. Then his dark eyes drooped and closed and the sleep of exhaustion claimed him once more.

He accepted the loss of his arm with an imperturbable coolness. After about a week, his strength rapidly flowing back and with it his wry sense of humor, he was actually joking about it with the nurses. And they, one and all, fell for his good looks and the light thing he made of being maimed, playing truant to pop in and out of his room during the day, to see him and have a brief, laughing chat with him. They called him "the pirate" and they all openly envied Fay.

She came every day; she never missed. Kate Ransome had insisted she stay on with her and Fay was frankly glad to fall in with the suggestion, for Kate's house was much nicer than a hotel would have been.

The news had quickly reached the papers that Lew Marsh had been an injured passenger on the train and Fay suddenly found herself dealing with phone calls, and telegrams of sympathy, all the way from Hollywood, with an efficient self-assurance that amazed her.

There had been one long-distance phone call from — of all people — Thalia Van Deen. Fay had turned to

Lew to ask what she should say in answer to Thalia's bitter-sweet demand for a few words from him to put in her column.

"Tell her to go lose herself in the Grand Canyon," he retorted lazily. "Or, better still, tell her to go to hell."

"Thalia," Fay said into the phone, smiling at the look of distaste on Lew's face, "Lew says it's very nice of you to phone." Her smile spread as he began to look indignant. "Oh, he's a lot better, thanks. What does he say? Oh, he says it could have been his head. Yes, really! I agree with you, he has got guts, hasn't he? Of course you can quote me. Oh, I really can't say when he'll be coming home, but he's definitely on the mend now. Yes, I was extremely lucky, wasn't I? The cause of the accident? I can't really say — there's to be an investigation, of course, but everyone here seems to think that the fog we had that night was the main cause. Oh, it was a hellish experience! Thank God the train wasn't packed — enough poor devils were killed and injured as it was. . . ."

When she finally replaced the phone, Lew said, "Why do you always have to be so soft with everyone — especially her sort?"

She shrugged. "It doesn't cost me anything, Lew," she replied.

He watched her then he turned his eyes from her. "You're too damned good to live!" he retorted.

And that was the closest he had come, in these weeks of his in hospital, to a remark that could be construed as personal. He openly showed her that he was grateful she stayed on in this little town called Farmer's Corner to be with him; coming to the hospital every day; writing his letters and handling his phone calls; bringing him amusing little presents, but his eyes never revealed anything more than gratitude and there were nights when Fay lay sleepless, wondering about the future — fearing the future.

Were they still as they had been before the crash? Was ultimate separation from him all she had to look forward to? Had she, perhaps, only dreamed the passionate purpose that had blazed in his eyes when he had leaped across that railway compartment; only imagined the exultation that had leapt like flame in them when he had reached her and torn her from her seat and had her close to him as they descended together into the maelstrom?

Bending to flick a small piece of fluff off the side of one of her navy suede shoes, she said, "I bet you can't wait for Saturday to come, can you, Lew? I was as pleased as anything when Dr. Ransome told me you were being discharged."

"Sure I'm pleased," he said, but abruptly he was frowning, looking away from her, out over the grounds of the hospital, where white-coated doctors strolled in the sunshine and patients and visitors sat talking on benches.

"Oh, I know you'll be sorry to leave your harem," she laughed.

He merely gave a rather moody shrug of his shoulders and she left the rail of the veranda and crossed to him. She put her hand upon his shoulder. "What's the matter, Lew?" she asked.

"Oh, nothing!" he said. "I guess I'm just a bit — well, everyone'll make such a damn fuss. That crowd back on the coast! You know what they are? They'll treat this empty sleeve like the book of the month!"

Her hand tightened on his shoulder. "They'll only mean it kindly, Lew."

"Sure, I know that," he agreed, "but they dramatize everything right out of proportion. This has happened — I've accepted it. But if anyone comes up to me and says, 'How too, too terrible, dear boy!', I'll sock him one." He gave her a brief moody smile. "So help me, Fay, I will!"

"You say that now, but once you're home again you'll feel differently." Fay's smile was reassuring.

"Maybe I'll change my mind and not go home," he retorted. "Now I come to think of it, I've all the world to choose from."

"But there's your work, Lew!" Now Fay regarded him with a dawning anxiety. "*Lucrece* is due for its Hollywood première — didn't Karl Christbel cable to tell you? You can't let the film down, Lew."

"Can't I?" He shrugged his wide shoulders. "Don't you know, Fay, that once a film is in the can, the director ceases to be of much importance to it? *Lucrece* will stand on its own merits. I think — I think I might go back to Toledo for a while. It's a fascinating place." He leaned his back against the back of his chair and screwed his eyes against the sunshine that was beating down warmly upon the veranda. "Toledo in September should be quite a place. I might rent a little house—stay till Christmas, then come home to be uncle to Dell's baby."

"Talking of Della's baby," Fay searched her purse with a hand that shook slightly, "I had a letter from her this morning." She found and opened the letter.

"The baby's doing fine. Della says he's showing signs of being a bit of a flirt." She read from the letter:

Tell Lew that his small namesake has definitely inherited his flirtatious tendencies, much to Will's discomfort. He smiles at all the women and merely blows bubbles at anything in pants. He's a real poppet, even though I do say so myself, all delicious brown skin and big brown eyes, a real Marsh. I did think he'd have Will's mop of flames, but he looks like he'll be as dark as I am. He's a darling! I'm longing for you to see him. When Will came to see Lew did he tell you that we've had the old rose arbor turned into a playhouse for the baby? It was Will's

174

idea. It looks fine. We've put in a swing and a little roundabout and had the walls painted all over with Walt Disney characters; you'd never recognize it for the old derelict it used to be. Now on the level, Fay, you're going to love this cute kid of mine; he talks with his eyes, so do bring Lew, just as soon as he's well enough to come, and doubtless when he sees Will's son and heir —

Fay broke off, the quick pink of confusion washing into her face. She avoided Lew's eyes as she returned the letter to her bag. "He sounds a stunning baby, doesn't he?" she said, fighting to keep her voice steady.

"Why shouldn't he be?" Lew was watching, carefully watching, the sudden little flags of color flying in Fay's cheeks — and he knew a quick, sharp pain that it should hurt her, perhaps embarrass her, that light remark of Dell's at the end of her letter. There came sweeping back over him the memory of Fay in the bedroom of that little pub at Thame . . . and wildly he pushed that memory from him, cloaking it in mockery.

"Dell's rather a stunner herself. Poor kid, she was quite upset, wasn't she, that our domestic ship had not drifted into safe harbor with hers and Will's. Dell, I fear, is inclined to forget that I'm a mere pirate, while her Will is a steady captain."

Fay listened to him with pain, turning from him so that he might not read her pain, which seemed to hold her heart in a fist shod with mail. She wanted to cry out to him, "Oh, my dear, we both made mistakes in the guiding of our ship. You wanted less than I was prepared to give. I wanted more than you could give."

When she did speak she said, "Lew, I don't quite know what you want me to do about — about Saturday. I mean — if you're not going home—"

175

"Don't worry about me, Fay," he carelessly rejoined..

"But naturally I'm worried! I'm worried about how you'll manage on your own." Fay stood tense by the rail of the veranda, her hands clenched on her bag. "Will you go to a hotel?"

"Sure." He continued to speak with carelessness. "I'll get room service to dress me and ask the waiter to clean the spilled soup off my waistcoat." He was smiling quizzically as Fay swung round to him, but when he saw the white torment of her face, his smile died. "Don't look like that — I was only joking." His hand moved, almost as though he would stretch it out to her, then it fell again to his rug-covered lap. "I've tied you to my bedside too many weeks already; I want you to fly away into the sun now, honey."

"Into the sun?" She was at a loss, her wide blue eyes fixed upon his face.

"Into the sun, my dear. Spreading your wings, flying far from the dark web I spread for you. Forget me — forget me very quickly; you'll be doing yourself a favor."

"Lew — don't!" The words broke from Fay. "Don't talk like that!"

"It's the truth, isn't it?" He spoke crisply, leaving himself no margin for excuse. "From this day I'll take no more of your compassion or your time. I'll be perfectly all right on my own."

"That isn't true and you know it, Lew!" Suddenly Fay was rather angry with him. The idea! Imagining he could stroll out into the world with that one arm and find no difficulties for himself! Her heels rang on the stone of the veranda as she crossed over to him. "About Saturday." Now it was her turn to speak with crisp decision. "I think you ought to go home, and no nonsense about it. I'll come with you — yes, Lew, I'll come with you. Let's say because I'm a soft-hearted fool who won't see you stumbling around on your own, trying to look after yourself. I'll come back with you and I'll be that other arm of yours until you're more able to cope. And if you tell me again that you want no more of my compassion or my time, I'll hit you over the head with this bag."

He gazed up at her, a reluctant little smile breaking on his mouth. "I believe you would paste me one, too," he murmured.

"I would!" She brandished the bag. "It's English leather, and English leather has plenty of body in it."

"But, honey, I want to go to Toledo." He spoke a trifle sulkily, like a small boy denied a toy.

"Don't be foolish!" She touched and shook his shoulder. "In a little while you'll be perfectly well and able to go anywhere you please, but at the moment you're still pretty helpless — and you know it, even though you won't admit it!"

At these words, his derisive grin danced on the edge of his mouth. "You sound like Nurse Joyce," he mocked. "I hope you intend to coddle me like she does. She's a champion coddler."

"Then you'll be sensible and go home on Saturday?"

"Yes, nurse."

Fay looked relieved.

Then, somewhere within the hospital, a strident little bell began to ring; the bell that warned visitors their time was almost up. Fay pulled on her gloves. "I'd better be off," she said, "or I shall have your pretty Nurse Joyce out here after me. I'll come again tomorrow, Lew. Oh, and I left some rum and butter toffees on your bedside locker, along with that J. B. Priestley novel you wanted to read."

"Thank you, Fay." He watched her go — was still watching the door through which she had disappeared when Dr. Ransome stepped out upon the veranda and approached him. There was a lingering smile of unmistakable pleasure on the young doctor's thin, olive-tinted face. "I've just seen your wife, Mr. Marsh," he said. "She isn't only a very plucky girl, she's also a very nice one."

Lew eyed him quizzically. "Plucky? Why, because she married me?"

The doctor looked surprised. "No," he said. "I was referring to the way she worked to save your bacon the night of the train wreck." His eyes narrowed. "Didn't you know? You'd have bled to death if it hadn't been for her presence of mind. She applied the crudest but the most efficient tourniquet I've ever seen and she helped me remove that arm of yours as calmly as though we were working together in an operating theatre instead of in the rubble of a wrecked train." He smiled, gravely, "Blood on her face, even on her hair, and the most determined little chin you ever saw in your life! That will-o'-the-wisp fought like ten tall men to save your life that night."

Lew's face had gone strangely still, but his eyes were blazingly alive, full of such raw shock that David Ransome abruptly ceased to smile and reached out to grip his shoulder. "What is it, man? What's up?" he demanded.

"Why should she — do all that, d'you think?" Lew murmured, huskily.

"Lord, she'd do it for anyone," the doctor explained. "She's the type."

"Of course." Lew nodded. He sank back in his chair, closing his eyes against the sun that shone into them. Blood on her face, even on her hair — he could see her, fighting for him, determined to hold back death; holding it back because once she had loved him, or holding it back because she had been trained to do so, and because it was as natural in her to relieve suffering as it was for her to breathe.

CHAPTER EIGHTEEN

As Fay and Lew crossed the quiet lobby of Crystal Court that Saturday evening of their return to Hollywood, Lew said casually, "Where shall we go for dinner? Have you any particular preference?"

She glanced up at him, a trifle embarrassed. "As a matter of fact, Lew, I'm going over to see the Forresters. I wrote Mimi, Max's wife, that I'd call in on them as soon as I got back to Hollywood. I'll probably have dinner there."

"Max Forrester's that doctor friend of yours, isn't he?"

She nodded. "He and Mimi are very nice. I got friendly with them while I was working at the Anita Hill. They've three of the jolliest kiddies you ever saw. Rollo, the youngest, has hair like white gold."

"Sounds cute." Lew's eyes rested on Fay's own very fair hair as they stepped into the lift; the soft curls glinted around a dark red hat and she looked, he thought, like some jaunty little pixie. He stood beside her in the lift, longing to touch those funny little boy's curls, yet vigorously restraining himself. She was not his to touch any more, though she stood with him now in this lift that carried them up to the apartment they had once shared so intimately.

His mouth pulled wryly. She was only here because he needed a nursemaid; someone to fix his tie, to lace his shoes, to cut up his dinner, but he'd soon learn to do these things for himself, and then she would go. Just as soon as he got used to living comfortably with one arm, he knew that she would bid him goodbye.

The lift ceased to ride and they stepped out. While Lew unlocked the door of the apartment, Fay — it was an old remembered habit — stood gazing out of the corridor window at the evening-bound streets, the flashing lights that spangled the tall buildings. Lew watched her a moment. Then he called out, "Come on, dreamer. You'll be late for your date with those friends of yours."

When she turned to him, something a little melancholy lurking beneath his smile caught her eye. "Would you — rather I came out with you?" she asked.

He shook his head. "Not on your life! I wouldn't spoil your evening for the world. You've spent enough time coddling me in the last few weeks; you go out and have some fun."

He switched on the light in the apartment and as he put down his suitcase and watched Fay carry hers into the room, his smile went and irritation claimed his mouth. "Dammit, Fay, I don't like to see you lugging that thing about!" he exclaimed.

She laughed. "Don't be so silly. I'm not a rabbit, even if I look like one." She put down the case and came over to him. She touched his arm tentatively. "Lew — would you — would you like to come to the Forresters' with me?" She knew she was a fool to ask. He'd only look scornful and laugh off her suggestion, but she felt strongly moved to ask him. The thought of leaving him to go out and seek a solitary dinner in a club, where people would stare and offer the condolences he dreaded, touched off her pity and gave her the courage to speak.

But he didn't say anything, he just stood staring at her.

She retreated a little from him, his silence confounding her. "They're awfully nice people — I just thought — I just thought you might like to come."

"I'd very much like to come," he said at last. His smile flashed warmly. "It's very nice of you to ask me, Fay."

"Oh — good!" She laughed, breathless with relief. "They won't mind a bit, they love company. And I rather thought you didn't much like the idea of dining out alone."

His face assumed a sardonic expression. "I must admit I wasn't exactly looking forward to having to ask the waiter to cut up my meat."

Her heart ached at his words, but she replied to him jocularly, "You could always pick your meat up in your hand and gnaw it like a caveman, Lew." She took up her suitcase. "I'm having the spare bedroom, aren't I?"

"Naturally!" He smiled slightly. "It's good of you to want to help me like this, Fay, but I can't help worrying a little about your job. You were longing to get back to it, I remember."

She shrugged. "I can always get another job. Nurses are always in demand."

"Even by incapacitated husbands, it would seem," he drawled.

She smiled. "I'm going to freshen up before we go to the Forresters'; I feel a bit messy after that long train journey." She walked towards the door of the spare bedroom, but at the door she turned to eye him a trifle severely. "Don't forget to call out if you want me for anything. It's what I'm here for. You will, won't you, Lew?"

"Cross my heart!" he promised. But as she disappeared into the room and the door closed, his smile faded, an abrupt look of weariness replacing it. He tossed his overcoat from him and crossed to the sideboard, pouring himself a straight whiskey. He drank it down quickly, wincing at the raw burn of it.

Why had he agreed to go to the Forresters'? Not because he didn't like the idea of eating alone, not because he was afraid of making a fiasco of eating in a public place, but because he wanted to be with Fay. That was the plain unvarnished truth — and he knew it. He was crazy about her! He could feel his heart pounding as he stood by the sideboard. He had not known himself capable of such feeling as this, grabbing him by the throat, making him ache with the effort not to go to her and beg her pardon for not loving her long, long ago.

He wanted her — how he wanted her, but still her pity was not enough; still it held him back. Had he not seen that pity exercised again tonight; seen it plain in her eyes when she had asked him if he would care to go and see these friends of hers?

Beware of pity! He scorned pity. He wanted her love. The sweet, warm love he had blasted to atoms with his brutality!

He glanced at his empty sleeve and an ironical smile moved about his mouth. He remembered the dark, scowling gypsy who had pierced the veil that enshrouded the future and seen him as he stood now. She had smiled and thought the loss of his arm the joke of fate. The loss of Fay's love was the joke of fate.

He sighed harshly. Doubtless he had earned the joke!

Fay rang the doorbell of the Forresters' house, smiling at Lew as they stood in the lighted porchway. "There's no need to look as though you're calling on your dentist," she murmured.

"I feel a little like it," he rejoined.

Then the door opened and Max Forrester stood framed against the hall lights, burly and blond, an expression of surprise on his face as he examined Lew.

"I hope I'm not the skeleton at the feast?" Lew said, following Fay into the house. He held out his hand to Max. "I'm Lew Marsh."

Max's eyes took in the pinned left sleeve, revealed under the lightweight coat as Lew shook hands. He met the steady friendly smile Lew was offering him, and he did a quick mental readjustment. He had been prepared to dislike this fellow heartily, if ever he should meet him, considering that any man who could hurt Fay had to be pretty despicable; but now, looking at that empty sleeve, remembering Fay's detailed account of the train crash in a letter to Mimi, he felt animosity die in him. This handsome devil couldn't be entirely despicable; the deep love Fay had once borne him proved it in some measure, while his spontaneous leap to shield her from hurt had been an act of selfless gallantry that definitely commended itself to the very masculine Max.

"Come along in and meet Mimi," Max said.

Mimi had heard the stranger's voice and she was standing up when they entered the sitting room, an enquiring expression on her face. Fay smiled as she walked across to her and kissed her cheek. "I brought Lew with me," she said. "I hope it's all right?"

"Of course." Mimi was a little overawed by the dark, smiling man who even foreshortened her own powerfully built Max. "Are you quite well now, Mr. Marsh?" she asked.

"In the pink," he replied, and his eyes, that couldn't help examining pretty women with pleasure, openly showed her that he thought her extremely pretty. Color moved in Mimi's cheeks and she understood now why Fay had once said that she had been as incapable of resisting Lew Marsh's charm as a kitten is incapable of resisting the muddling and entwining wiles of a ball of wool.

"Here, let me take your coat," Max said to him, and Lew shrugged out of it, handing it to him with a murmur of thanks. His glance had settled on a squat teddy-bear astride the radio, one orange ear comically askew

183

and a pink paper skirt about his middle. He grinned at Mimi. "Fay tells me you've got three boys, Mrs. Forrester," he said.

"Three loads of mischief," she amended. "Now they're all tucked up in bed, sleeping the innocent sleep of the righteous." She indicated a chair. "Please sit down," she said. "What do you drink?"

"Tomato juice," Fay called across from the other side of the room, where she was handing her coat to Max.

Lew settled back in his armchair, his eyes moving over the laughing Fay as she emerged from her coat. She wore pleated coral-pink linen that made her look as cleanly slender as a boy. "Ignore her, Mrs. Forrester," he said to Mimi. "She's one of those poor Puritan souls who get giddy on orangeade. She's to be pitied really."

Mimi laughed as she mixed drinks. "I'm going to give you a concoction of Max's," she said. "And do call me Mimi."

"Right you are!" he said at once, smiling at Fay as she came across the room to him. She perched herself on the arm of his chair, reaching down to pull his tie a little straighter. "I don't do these half as well as you used to," she spoke apologetically. "I'm not much of a valet, I'm afraid, Lew."

"You're not doing too badly," he murmured, watching her bent head, thinking how lovely, how tender, she was.

Mimi brought drinks to them, her eyes widening at the picture of Fay, leaning over this dark, self-assured, rather over-powering person, casually adjusting his tie for him.

Lew accepted his drink and sipped at it, nodding reflectively. "Um, pretty potent!" His dark eyes sparkled into Mimi's. "Trying the same on Fay?" he enquired.

"No, Mimi isn't," Fay said, accepting her drink, which was obviously the much maligned orangeade.

Dinner was extremely good and afterward they just talked, a pleasant flow of conversation, relaxing and curiously enjoyable. Lew was amazed at the extent of his own enjoyment. He liked this well lived-in room, with its deep, easy chairs, its spot of crayon scribbling low down on one of the walls, its comical teddy-bear perched on the radio, liked the way Fay and Mimi ate chocolate drops with the ease of kids at a picnic.

Fay was fully revealed to him in this comfortable, friendly house — and the revelation delighted him. She was quite without shyness, unafraid to be herself, and once, when Mimi heard one of the children cry out in the nursery, she begged to be allowed to go up to him. "It's Rollo, isn't it?" she said. "Do let me go up, Mimi. I'll soon get him back to sleep."

Mimi laughed. "Go on, then, as it's Rollo. I know he's your dreamboat."

Fay hurried from the room and Max said, proffering Lew a light for his cigar, "Do you have any trouble with what's left of that arm?"

Lew considered. "I sometimes," he said, "get the oddest feeling that I've still got a hand. I go to use it. I actually feel as though I can move my fingers. Weird, isn't it?"

"You'll lose that sensation by and by," Max said. "It's early days yet. Will you try an artificial limb, later on?"

"Oh no!" Lew laughed, somewhat ruefully. "I want no phoney attachments, thanks! I'll manage."

Max nodded. "I'd feel the same myself," he admitted.

When Fay returned from the nursery her face was dimpled with a lingering amusement. "No wonder he couldn't sleep," she announced. "He had a fire-engine in the bed with him. A gruesome thing, with ladders

185

jutting out all over it. I had a hard job persuading him to exchange it for a woolly dog."

"What argument did you employ?" Max enquired, looking interested.

She came across the room and resumed her seat on the arm of Lew's chair. "I had to tell him a terribly sentimental doggy story. Mind you," her dimples were well to the fore, "he didn't believe a word of it. You know Rollo."

Max looked fond but quizzical. "I certainly do know Rollo." He glanced at Lew. "Takes after his mother, that laddie does. Hasn't an ounce of sentimentality in him."

"That isn't true!" Mimi protested. "Don't be mean, Max. Look at the way I cried over that movie we saw last week."

"What movie was that?" Lew asked, with quick interest.

"Oh, quite an old one," Mimi said, "a re-issue, I think. It was called *Irene Abbott*".

Fay turned in quick eagerness to Lew, smiling down at him. "That's one of yours, isn't it, Lew? Surely I've heard you mention it? Of course I have! I saw it while I was at Casa Roche, nursing your grandmother. I mentioned how much I'd enjoyed it and you said, then, that you had directed it."

"I did direct it, honey." His eyes smiled into her blue eyes, so candid and lovely, the fair lashes glinting as they curled back. Then he turned to Mimi. "I must admit I still get a kick out of hearing someone say they've enjoyed that movie. It's still one of my most successful ventures."

"I loved that ending," Mimi said. "The way the rain fell in one great sheet as Irene fled down the drive of that awful house. And that final moment on the cliff edge!" Mimi gave a little shiver of reminiscent pleasure. "Why did she have to die, though? Why

186

couldn't you have let her husband reach her in time?"

"And spoil one of the best shots in the film?" Lew demanded, looking amused. "I couldn't resist letting Irene jump off that cliff in the pelting rain. Stupendous stuff!"

"You are cold-blooded, Lew!" Fay protested.

"I might tell you," he said, "that I was very tempted to let the husband follow Irene to her murky death."

"He didn't love her enough," Fay declared. "It wouldn't have rung true. It's a good job you didn't give way to your temptation."

"That's true," Mimi agreed. "He didn't love her enough to die with her. You'd have spoiled the film."

"The point is," Max put in, taking his pipe from his mouth and using it to emphasize his words, "would a man, standing on the brink of death, think: 'This is love, I must follow!'? Would that be a natural reaction? He might reach out, automatically, to save the woman, but if he failed, would he really want to follow her to her death?"

"A spontaneous action," Lew said quietly, "is never truly comprehended. It arises from a primitive desire for self-preservation, or from an equally primitive desire for self-sacrifice. Such an action wouldn't necessarily be motivated by love. Even a man passionately in love might balk at dying with his mate, might in the moment of crisis find himself preserving his own life at the expense of the woman's. I honestly believe that it's a purely primitive reaction. A man could leap, quite without thinking, to save the life of a complete stranger."

"Possibly," Max murmured. "But that would surely depend on whether or not the man in question was interested enough in his fellow creatures to put himself out to save one of them, or die for one of them. Not every man has such an overwhelming love of mankind. He'd surely have to be that type, wouldn't he, to leap

187

so spontaneously to preserve the life of a complete stranger?"

Lew was watching Max, a sudden wariness in his eyes. This blond doctor was trying to drive him into a corner, trying to get him to say something that would reveal his own motive in leaping to shield Fay — to shield her or die with her.

That hadn't been natural love of mankind! That had been sheer, primitive desire to be with her in a moment of racking horror, to go down into the bowels of hell with her, or to fly straight up through the gates of heaven. It hadn't mattered which, just so long as they were together, that slender body one with his through all their days and nights in eternity. That was all he had wanted, and he had known it, as he had dived to claim her.

He said now to Max, "If we examined all our actions and what motivates them, we'd spend half our lives on a psychiatric couch." He smiled lazily, "I'll leave Freud to you. I'll take plain D. H. Lawrence. I understand his philosophy a whole lot better."

When Fay and Lew had gone and Max returned to the sitting room, Mimi, who was collecting up glasses, swung round to him. Her eyes were eager. "What do you think, Max? Do you think they'll stay together?"

Max shrugged his shoulders, lounging at ease against the mantelpiece. "Fay's a soft-hearted little coot; she may not be able to walk out on him. Did she say she was going to?"

"She said she was only staying with him until he's more able to manage with that one arm." Mimi came across the room to her husband and with a gesture of complete trust in his love burrowed her face into his broad chest. "Did you like him, Max?" she asked.

Max lightly touched her smooth dark hair. "Yes, honey, I did. He's been through quite a bit of hell, and it's knocked off the sharp edges, fined him down."

"I thought that." Mimi drew a quick little sigh. "Oh, I do hope they stay together! He must be awfully fond of her — he lost an arm for her, didn't he?" Then Mimi's eyes slowly widened as she remembered the look she had surprised on Lew's face — that look of unmistakable worship, softening away his arrogance, flooding warm and tender in his eyes as he had watched Fay's fair head bent close to his breast, her hands at his tie. "Do you know what I think?" Mimi declared. "I think that mixed-up guy is crazy about Fay."

She heard Max laugh and glanced up at him. "I do, Max," she asserted.

"Honey, am I arguing with you?" he laughed.

Going home in the cab, Fay said to Lew, "You liked the Forresters, didn't you?" She smiled. "You looked surprised. What did you expect?" She watched his face in the passing lamplight, saw his rather embarrassed expression. "They've no sophistication, no brittle pretensions. They're just real nice. Two of the nicest people I've ever known."

"Your sort, eh?" he drawled, amused and touched by her staunch support of Max and Mimi. "No enamelled glamor. No blazé wit! No vicious ambition."

"No." She laughed, laying her head back against the leather of the cab. "Just relaxed and pleasant and absolutely straight. My sort, as you say." Then, as she lay like that, resting her head, she yawned a little and apologetically covered her mouth with her hand. "I guess I'm a little tired," she said. "Aren't you tired, Lew? This is your first full day out of hospital, after all."

He shook his head. "I've spent so many hours in bed in the last few weeks, I'm only too thankful to be back on my feet."

"The harem looked pretty crestfallen when we left," Fay remarked, smiling.

"I didn't notice David Ransome doing any dance of mad delight," Lew retorted. "When you shook hands with the poor guy I thought he was going to burst into tears." He watched her as he spoke. Her complete unawareness of her own delicate appeal fascinated him. She had no tricks; no flirtatious mannerisms. She just looked sweet and clean; dipped in dew, like an early morning flower, he reflected, smiling at his own lapse into poetic romanticism.

And suddenly he was uncertain of himself. How was he going to keep from reaching out after her, when he wanted her so much? Already he was longing to touch quiet fingers to that thin, sweet cheek, those boyish curls, and he doubted his ability to suppress that longing indefinitely. It wouldn't be easy, having to see her around the apartment, acting the impersonal nursemaid, the courteous little friend. It wouldn't be at all easy.

"I like Dr. Ransome a lot," Fay murmured. "He's a very genuine sort of person."

"Would it surprise you to learn that I liked him myself?" Lew laughed slightly. "I didn't get the urge to wring his neck every time he looked at you, like I used to with Jerry Kaufmann."

"To wring his neck! Dr. Ransome's neck?" The words came in a hurrying surprise from Fay. "I'm nothing to you, Lew, so why should you want to do that?"

"You're only all the world and every moment I shall spend in eternity." Then he sat up sharply, realizing what he had said. "Ignore that Fay." Now he spoke crisply. "It's like a cheap line from a movie."

"Not cheap!" Suddenly she was clutching his arm. "Not cheap, but worth a terrible lot, if you meant it."

A tense silence followed her words, then, almost blindly, Lew reached for her — and the moment he touched her, blown sky-high was his resolve to hide his love and his longing. "I couldn't bear to take pity from you," he whispered, "but if you've anything else to offer me, my darling, I'll take it with both hands — grovelling on my knees."

"Lew!" She held his face in her hands, incredulous with delight. "Darling, you don't have to grovel." Then her arms were about his neck, tight and close. "My dear pirate, I'd hate to see you grovelling." She laughed tremulously. "It wouldn't suit you."

"You call me your 'dear pirate'," his arm tightened about her, almost convulsively, "but don't forget how I've hurt you."

"Hush!" She stroked his black hair, gentle with him in her love, though pulses throughout her small body were leaping with exultant life at his warm, masculine closeness. Gone was the stranger she had said goodbye to in England; she had never really known that Lew, but this one was different — this one was telling her he loved her. "Nothing that happened before this moment matters," she whispered. "This is all that matters, this love we've found together."

"But you said — you said you could only be happy apart from me. I want your happiness, Fay. I don't want to be the cause of any more pain to you." He pressed his face to her; breathed the faint perfume of her dress, felt the warm race of her heart under his cheek. "You're so lovely — so sweet! How can I let you go?"

"I don't want you to let me go." A husky little laugh broke from her. "I was very foolish to say that I could only be happy apart from you. I don't live or feel or want when I'm apart from you. I'm a mere automaton, minus her mainspring." She laughed again. "Tell me you don't want me merely to valet you."

"I just want you, my very dear angel!" Lingeringly, then, he kissed her mouth; her lovely mouth, that he hadn't known for long, harsh months. With delight and wonder he stepped into the sweet, warm world of her love again. When he finally lifted his head and she. snuggled to him with a little murmur of supreme content, he said, "Fay, do you know what I'm going to buy you?"

"You and your presents!" She laughed against his warm throat. "Darling, I don't want a present."

"You'll want this one." His lips were against her forehead, where the fine, soft curls stirred under his breathing. "I'm going to buy you a house. Something alive and friendly, like that house of the Forresters', with an enormous garden. What do you say?"

For a moment she was too choked to say anything. Now she knew that in his full reading of her heart and its desires, he truly loved her. Now she knew that no dark clouds would fly over that house he would buy for her; that he would make only sunshine for her. Very tenderly she kissed his cheek. "I'll let you live in it with me, if you like, my dear," she said.